Escape from Fort Benton

Nathan Palmer and Jeff Morgan happen across an ambush too late to help the victims, but a dying man gives them a gun, a key and a cryptic message about 10,000 dollars being available in Fort Benton in five days' time.

Now Nathan and Jeff set about getting their hands on the money. However, Fort Benton is the private empire of Mayor Decker and his ruthless form of justice. Before the day is out the pair are beaten up and thrown in jail.

In Decker's clutches, they're going to need all their courage if they are ever to escape.

Escape from Fort Benton

Scott Connor

A Black Horse Western

ROBERT HALE · LONDON

ISBN-10: 0-7090-8120-0
ISBN-13: 978-0-7090-8120-3

Robert Hale Limited
Clerkenwell House
Clerkenwell Green
London EC1R 0HT

Typeset by
Derek Doyle & Associates, Shaw Heath
Printed and bound in Great Britain by
Antony Rowe Limited, Wiltshire

CHAPTER 1

'I tell you,' Nathan Palmer said, 'that just has to be gunfire.'

Nathan's fellow-rider Jeff Morgan glanced up and down the trail, flinching as another sharp but distant blast sounded, then echoed back from the bluff behind him.

'You're right,' he said, 'but where's it coming from?'

Nathan pointed to a monolithic outcrop of rock ahead, a single slim finger aiming up to the heavens.

'I'm guessing from beyond that rock.'

'I reckon you're right.' Jeff drew his horse to a halt then turned it round and headed back towards the bluff.

Nathan looked over his shoulder at Jeff's receding back.

'Where you going?' he shouted after him.

'When there's gunfire ahead and we ain't the target,' Jeff called over his shoulder, 'I go back the way I came.'

Nathan opened his mouth to argue, but then another volley of shots rang out and this time the rapidity of the firing suggested that at least three people were involved. That was all the encouragement Nathan needed. He hurried his horse on, heading for the outcrop.

Jeff shouted after him, but he ignored his friend's calls for him to not be so reckless. He rode on until he reached the base of the outcrop, then drew his horse to a halt. He dismounted and tethered his horse then looked back. Over a hundred yards of dusty trail, the two men stared at each other.

Nathan saw Jeff's mouth move as he muttered silently to himself, but just as Nathan turned away to climb up the slope, with a resigned shake of his head Jeff shook the reins and headed after him.

Bent forward at the waist and with his hands frequently grabbing at rocks to steady himself, Nathan fought his way up through the loose shale. He climbed up on a route that took him to the side of the finger of rock.

When the area beyond opened up to his view, he flopped on his belly and saw that the situation was broadly as he'd imagined it from hearing the gunfire. A red-coated man was trading shots with two other men. They had all found cover behind boulders, but from his high position, Nathan caught glimpses of each hunched and huddled person. Two dead men were sprawled on the ground.

He reckoned he could pin the men down, but from over a hundred yards away, he was unlikely to hit a target. He needed to get closer to be more effective. Several boulders at the bottom of the slope would provide cover, but to reach them he'd have to run for at least fifty yards down the slope, all the time in full view.

On his own the act would be too risky, but he was pleased to hear Jeff shuffle up the slope to join him. Jeff darted up to consider the scene then lay back down.

'Satisfied your curiosity?' he asked.

'I wasn't curious,' Nathan said. 'I came to help.'

'That helpful attitude was always sure to get you in trouble one day.' Jeff patted his arm then pointed back to their horses. 'Now, come on. This ain't got nothing to do with us.'

Nathan leaned back to consider his sandy-haired friend, searching for the words that would persuade him to stay. Jeff had six inches on him and the powerful hams of his hands meant he was someone who could take care of himself. But contrary to, or perhaps because of, his appearance as an easily angered fighting man, he was reluctant to get involved in a skirmish. Although once he got involved he could always be relied upon to end it.

'You're right. This ain't our business,' Nathan said, gesturing back down the slope. 'But we got to be able to do something, surely.'

'And what's that? We don't even know who's in the right here.'

Nathan didn't want to admit that Jeff was right and he reviewed the scene again. He noticed that to his left three horses were standing by a seep, the clawed-away dirt suggesting the men had dug down for a while before they'd found water. The horses of the men to the right had mooched off a distance.

He pointed. 'I reckon those men to the left were watering their horses and the others ambushed them. Now, the one remaining man is outnumbered and pinned down and he ain't getting out of here alive without our help.'

'You may be right, but you don't know that for sure.'

Jeff shuffled back a pace. 'Come on. Nobody's ever helped us out before and I don't see no reason why we should risk ourselves here.'

'And you know that's wrong.' Nathan fixed Jeff with his gaze until he lowered his head, then drew his gun. 'If you don't want to help that man, don't, but just wait until the other men see me, then cover me.'

Nathan drew his six-shooter and shuffled on to his haunches, steeling himself for slipping over the edge and hurrying down the slope. He took deep breaths to calm his churning guts and pattering heart.

In truth, he'd never faced a situation like this before. During the two years he and Jeff had been friends, they'd punched cows on cattle drives and so had been called on to see off rustlers and other troublemakers. But in those situations Nathan had always been with a large group and his quarries had always been fleeing. Now, he was on his own and his quarries were close and determined.

But last month he and Jeff had decided they'd had enough of being ordered around and they'd headed north out of Texas in search of a life beyond the endless cattle drives. They had now reached the Santa Fe Trail and although they were some twenty miles west of their destination of Fort Benton, he reckoned that happening across this ambush was as good a time as any to start seizing control of his life.

He crawled forward until the land dipped away then rolled over a shoulder and kept the roll going until he landed on his feet. Then, crouched over, he ran down the slope.

He'd hoped to get most of the way to the bottom before the men saw him, at which time he'd need Jeff's covering fire, but he was pleased to hear pounding foot-falls behind him as his friend followed.

As he ran, Nathan darted his gaze between the two men on the right and the red-coated man on the left, looking for their reaction. It was the men on the right who bobbed up first and saw him. Instantly, one man swung his gun round and fired up at him. On the run, Nathan returned gunfire. More gunfire sounded as Jeff also fired and even though all their shots were wild, the red-coated man used the distraction to blast at the man who had fired, forcing him to dive for safety.

Nathan put on a burst of speed and slid to a halt behind the nearest boulder. He slammed his gun on the top of the boulder and tore off three quick shots even though nobody was visible, then ducked as Jeff joined him.

'You followed,' he said, smiling as he reloaded.

Jeff shrugged. 'If you're going to act like a damn fool, I'd better act like one too. But I still don't know what you hope to achieve here.'

'Well, I reckon I've learnt one thing.' While keeping his head down, Nathan pointed towards the man who'd fired at him. 'One of the men I reckoned was an ambusher shot at us and that means he's in the wrong here.'

'Or he might be in the right and he thought we were even more people come to attack him.'

'Either way, he shot at us, and that makes him our enemy now.'

Jeff sighed, but then gave a reluctant nod.

'All right,' he said. He joined Nathan in slipping closer to the boulder then shuffled up on to his haunches while Nathan raised himself to peer over.

9

Beyond, all the men were staying low.

'Hey,' Nathan shouted, 'you people over there. What's this about?'

Nobody replied immediately, but again one of the men to the right reacted first. He edged up to look at them, then ducked.

'You some kind of lawmen?' he shouted.

'We . . .' Nathan looked at Jeff with his eyebrows raised, and Jeff shook his head. 'No, but we're here to help. So I reckon you should all just—'

'Stay out of this. It ain't got nothing to do with you.'

The man darted up and fired, the shot blasting into the boulder just inches to the side of Nathan's head and tearing grit into his cheek.

Nathan ducked, hearing a sustained burst of gunfire rip out. He glanced at Jeff, who gave a resigned head-shake that said he knew this would turn out badly, then he crawled along behind the boulder to the next one, to come up in a different position. He ventured a glance at the scene.

The situation had changed. The man had paid for shooting at him with a gunshot to the chest and was now lying sprawled face down over a rock. His colleague was standing, clutching a bleeding shoulder and firing at the other man who was running towards him. He fired with deadly accuracy, his shot scything into the running man's guts.

The man folded, his momentum letting him run on for three more faltering paces before he stumbled and keeled over into the dirt to lie face down. He twitched once then stilled.

Nathan looked at the other man, but he had turned to face him, his gun swinging round to aim at him.

Fuelled on by the intensity of the sudden fight, Nathan reacted instantly. He aimed and fired a moment before the other man did, his shot ploughing into the man's chest and throwing him backwards, the redirected return shot whistling high over Nathan's head.

Slowly, Nathan stood. He was sure everyone had been hit, perhaps fatally, but took no chances as he rounded the boulder then paced out into the open.

Jeff joined him, his gun drawn and darting round to aim at each boulder, but nobody emerged. Nathan went to the left and Jeff to the right, each man searching behind the rocks, but they returned to confirm that the only people here were in the open.

Nathan rolled the man he had tried to save on to his back, but he flopped down. The damp redness spreading across his red coat confirmed he was dead.

'Seems we didn't help none,' Jeff said, 'after all.'

'We tried and did our best,' Nathan said, hoping the words might help to convince Jeff as well as himself, but finding they sounded hollow.

He walked over to the man who had shot at him. The side of this man's head was gory and misshapen and Nathan didn't fancy confirming that he was dead.

But then he heard a sharp intact of breath from ahead.

Jeff hadn't made the sound and Nathan crouched down, glancing around.

His gaze alighted on the man he had shot. This man was lying facing away from him, his legs drawn up to his chest. Although his gun lay several feet from his body, Nathan told Jeff to keep a gun on him, then walked in a steady arc until he could see the man's face. He knelt a few feet away.

11

The man had his cheek pressed into the dirt as he looked up at Nathan.

'You shot me,' he said, his weak tone flat and devoid of bitterness.

'Only to stop you shooting me.'

The man moved his head, his flickering eyes suggesting he was trying to nod.

'Tell me . . .' A deep wince contorted his face and when his expression smoothed, his eyes were blank. 'Were . . . were you trying to help us or him?'

'Him.'

The man snorted. 'Then I had bad luck right up to the end.'

'You saying you didn't ambush those other men?'

The man didn't reply immediately and Nathan wondered whether he ever would, but then he rocked his head back. A whispered request emerged.

'Come closer.'

Nathan still didn't trust the dying man and he glanced at Jeff, signifying with a raised eyebrow that he should be on his guard. Then he shuffled closer, but stayed back far enough to watch the man's movements.

'What you want?' he asked.

'Go to Fort Benton,' the man murmured, his voice weak and faltering.

'We were going there anyway. Who do you want us to tell about this?'

'Nobody. Hide our bodies. Don't tell nobody nothing. No time to explain . . . No time . . .' The man twitched, rolling himself on to his back. Pain contorted his face into an ugly grimace. He coughed, bubbling blood over his lips. He raised a hand a few inches and gestured feebly to a horse before his hand flopped down to the dirt. 'It's in my saddle-bag. Take it.'

Nathan was now sure the man wasn't trying to lure him in to carry out a final act of revenge and he edged forward to look down at him.

'What's in there? And why?'

The man's eyes closed and Nathan couldn't hear him breathing any more. Nathan reached out, his fingers questing for the man's neck to check his pulse, but then the man drew in a rattling intake of breath and when he spoke again, his voice grated through every tortured word.

'By Wednesday . . . Wednesday . . . ten thousand dollars . . . Wednesday . . .' He uttered a strangulated grunt. His head slowly lolled to the side. Then the only sound was the wind rustling by and the only movement was the fluttering of the man's collar.

'Ten thousand dollars,' Jeff said from behind Nathan. 'And Wednesday. What you reckon that means?'

'I don't know.' Nathan stood. 'But we might find out more now.'

Nathan headed to the man's horse, removed the saddle-bag, and rummaged inside. Only one object was within, cold and heavy. Nathan removed it to find he was clutching the looping coil of a gunbelt and holster, laden with bullets and a Peacemaker initialled with the ornate letters FR. In the loop nearest the holster, a key dangled. The key was large and rusty and when Nathan slipped it from the belt and held it up for Jeff to take, it was so large it poked out of each side of his friend's giant fist.

'Wednesday,' Jeff mused, turning the key over. 'I guess he meant we got to find somewhere in Fort

Benton to use this key by Wednesday.'

'Or the gun.'

'Or both.'

Nathan considered then smiled. 'It's Friday today, so we got ourselves five whole days to do it.'

'Yeah,' Jeff said, 'and there's ten thousand dollars at stake if we can work out what we have to do.'

Jeff grinned and despite all the bodies around him, Nathan couldn't help but return the grin.

'There is.' He winked. 'And aren't you glad now you decided to help?'

CHAPTER 2

'Fort Benton is a mighty big place,' Jeff said, drawing his horse to a halt. 'Where do you reckon we start looking?'

Nathan leaned forward in the saddle, peering through the fort's large open gates, then shrugged.

'Perhaps we should just ride on in and listen out. We might overhear someone mention that something will happen next Wednesday, or ten thousand dollars, or something that'll give us a clue as to how we can use this key.'

Jeff nodded, and side by side they rode through the gates.

They had found no clues on the men's bodies to help them work out how the key could get them the money. Neither had they found any clues to suggest a reason for the gunfight or anything that'd confirm they'd taken the gunbelt and key from someone they could trust. And although both men were honest enough never to consider stealing, they agreed that they had to explore the possibility of getting their hands on so much money – provided they didn't have to deprive a decent person of his well-earned dollars.

They hadn't agreed on what they'd spend the money on if they did find it, aside from the fact that they'd set themselves up so they'd never have to punch cows again. But before they faced that problem they had to find it.

In the saloon they purchased warm beers and sat at a table by the door considering the fort.

It was as it'd been described to them last month when they'd made this their destination. It was a large adobe fort, the original buildings having been erected some forty years ago when it was a major trading site for Plains Indians and trappers. But when the US Army no longer had a need for this supply base the sprawling complex had fallen into disrepair. Even after many years of neglect, it was still a veritable castle on the plains, and now a home for the trading settlement that had sprung up both inside and outside the walls.

There was a large central parade-ground now baked hard under the relentless afternoon sun. In the shadows around the sides were walled spaces that had previously been offices, barrack-rooms, stables and which the townsfolk had now converted to a variety of uses, including the saloon.

The fort walls were higher than the rooms and were wide enough for two men to walk side by side. But they were no longer manned.

At the back of the parade-ground there was a complex of buildings dominated by the solid square block of the watch-tower, which was still an excellent look-out point to survey the surrounding landscape. The squat building to the side of the tower had become Mayor Decker's office. The windows in both the tower and the office were open spaces, the bars having long gone. But the bars in the windows of the other building beside the tower were still there, this being the jail-house and law office.

Aside from the two red-uniformed guards standing outside the large double doors at the base of the tower, the fort maintained a sleepy atmosphere. Few people were moving about in the afternoon heat, which suggested that their original hope of finding work here would turn out to be optimistic. And although enough businesses were here to suggest prosperity, the possibil-ity of $10,000 being available in a few days ought to have generated some interest. But as it was, they drank their beers and two more without them overhearing anyone talk about money or anything that would suggest a reason for the gunfight they'd encountered this morning.

Later, emboldened by liquor, Nathan returned his glasses to the bar and quizzed the bartender with what he hoped was a subtle question.

'Anything ever happen around here?' he asked, lean-ing on the bar. He kept his expression relaxed while his roving gaze avoided any display of interest in the answer.

The bartender considered him with a sullen lack of interest as a solitary fly buzzed lazily around him.

'Nope.'

'Something must happen sometimes, surely.'

The bartender rocked his head from side to side then raised a finger.

'Last week Sheriff Buckthorn brought in the man who shot Frank Reed. Aside from that, nothing.' He slapped a hand on the fly, crushing it to the bar. 'And that's the way we like it.'

Nathan nodded and beckoned for Jeff to join him.

'And so do we. Reckon as we might stop here – if we can find work.'

The bartender blew out his cheeks, shaking his head.

'Ain't much of that around.'

Nathan nodded and shuffled from side to side, pondering on his next question, but Jeff nudged him aside.

'But there's got to be something available,' Jeff said, slapping his large hands on the bar. 'Who's got all the money around here?'

A cold-eyed suspicious glare replaced the bartender's bored expression as he considered the hulking man before him.

'You ask a lot of questions, stranger.'

Nathan shot Jeff an admonishing glance for being so unsubtle, then spoke up.

'We're just eager to work.' He stood back from the bar and placed his hands wide, smiling. 'We just want to know who's got the resources to pay us a decent wage.'

'And your line of work?'

'Worked on cattle drives aplenty, but we've had a bellyful of that and we reckon as we can turn our hands to pretty much anything.' Nathan leaned forward. 'In fact, if you're looking for help, we might be interested.'

'I ain't.' The bartender shrugged, his sudden concern gone from his eyes as he pointed outside. 'But I guess you might find someone who'll hire two men who'll do anything, provided you knock on doors until you do find that someone.'

Nathan nodded, but Jeff grunted with irritation.

'But that could take for ever,' he grumbled. 'What we want to know—'

'We welcome your advice,' Nathan said, interrupting him, then he drew Jeff aside.

Jeff continued to grumble as they headed to the door. When they were outside he slammed his hands on his hips and loomed over Nathan.

'What you stop me asking him questions for?' he demanded.

'Because you weren't exactly being subtle.' Nathan stared up at him until his friend acknowledged this fact with a rueful smile.

'I guess I leave being subtle and being curious to you.' He slapped a large fist against his thigh. 'And I'll tell you one thing for sure – I don't like mysteries.'

'Then don't you worry, my friend. That bartender gave me an idea as to how we solve our mystery.' Nathan winked. 'And as it ain't subtle, I reckon you'll like it.'

'And what's that?'

Nathan didn't reply immediately as he considered the swinging batwings, noting that they were incapable of being locked, then roved his gaze past the deserted and doorless room beside the saloon until it rested on a store. This room had a large open door.

Nathan pointed. 'It's simple. You do what you did in the saloon and ask the storekeeper unsubtle questions about work. I'll do the rest.'

Jeff's gaze settled on the door to the store and he provided a low chuckle then a nod.

Five minutes later Jeff emerged from the store, shaking his head, and reported that the storekeeper didn't need help. Nathan reported that while Jeff was distracting the storekeeper, he'd discovered that the key didn't fit in the door to the store.

'I guess,' Jeff said with a sigh, 'we'll just have to try

again and keep on trying until we do find which door will accept the key.'

Nathan looked around the rooms surrounding the parade-ground, then up at the tower and lastly through the gates at the settlement beyond, totting up just how many buildings were here that could accept the key.

'And hopefully,' he murmured, 'we can try them all before Wednesday.'

For the next three hours Nathan and Jeff worked their way through every room around the parade-ground, then around the buildings outside the gates. They weren't successful. Most of the doors to the rooms within the fort were large and were sturdy enough to need a key the size of the one they had. But the buildings outside the fort were mainly clapboard shacks with no way to keep anyone out, not that they contained anything worth taking.

Nevertheless, they were methodical and tried everywhere. Each time, Jeff told the true tale of their search for work, as Nathan offered an untroubling smile while surreptitiously searching for a door, or anything, that could provide a home for the key in his pocket. If he saw a likely target, he'd flash Jeff a signal, and Jeff would take that as his cue to ramble on until he'd provided a distraction that'd let Nathan try the key in the lock he'd found.

But as the day wore on, Nathan's and Jeff's attentions increasingly returned to the central tower and its surrounding buildings. They had gathered no clues as to where they might be able to use the key, but few people passed by the centre of the fort. So they reckoned it was the kind of defendable location where someone might have hidden $10,000. If they were to back a hunch, they'd back the notion that the money would be in a room or perhaps in a casket or cabinet stored away in one of these buildings.

So they slowly arced their way in towards this area, considering the buildings from a variety of angles as they strolled around. As they walked past the jailhouse door they saw that the only way into the tower and mayor's office was through the double doors at the base of the tower. The two guards who stood beside this doorway watched them approach in a casual way, although Nathan reckoned this was a studied form of unconcern.

Opposite these buildings were the stables. At a steady pace they walked beside this building, considering the mayor's office and tower while debating in low but casual tones what they should do. They decided they should abandon the approach they had used so far. The guards might refuse to let them enter and afterwards they would view everything they did with suspicion. They needed to sneak into those buildings unseen.

Maintaining their casual stroll, they headed past the open door without looking at the doorway or the guards. Beyond the tower, a wall arced away from them and when they'd passed the stables, they crossed over to walk beside it until they were out of view of the guards. But they discovered that the wall met the main wall of the fort and in the area between the walls and beyond the stables and tower, there were no other buildings. They turned on the spot, running their gazes across the imposing, blank walls until they faced the back door to the stables, the only opening in the walls that they could see.

They had no choice but either to go into the stables

or return to the parade-ground. After a quick debate, they turned on their heels and headed back along the wall, approaching the tower.

It was then that they had a spot of luck. When the doorway to the tower swung back into view, a wagon had pulled up and both guards had their backs to them. One guard was talking to the driver while the other peered at the load on the back of the wagon.

With this sudden fortunate occurrence having distracted the guards, Nathan and Jeff hurried to the doorway, then side-stepped inside. Although he was hurrying, Nathan noted that the lock on the open doors was too large to accept the key.

They walked through a short tunnel, which opened out onto a plaza. It was the same rectangular shape as the parade-ground outside, but smaller. At the end of the plaza there was the ruined shell of a mission, the tower was to the left, another door to the jailhouse was to the right, and the mayor's office loomed over them above the doorway.

After looking around the plaza Nathan's gaze returned to the tower and the doorway that led to it. A flight of steps arced away from his view.

They glanced at each other, silently confirming their next actions, then paced to the steps and up them. The steps spiralled in a half-circle before opening up onto an area that was either a wide corridor or a long bare room. An open door at the end of this space led to the mayor's office.

They exchanged a few silent gestures and decided to explore this room after they'd been up to the tower. They turned to head up the next flight of steps. Nathan had climbed up the first step when a scraping, then a cough sounded behind him.

'There's nothing up there,' a voice intoned.

Nathan flinched, then took a deep breath to compose himself. He turned to face an imposing man, a trim moustache and steely eyes considering them from the doorway to the office.

'Mayor Decker?' Nathan asked.

'I am. How did you get in here?'

Nathan shrugged. 'We walked in through the door.'

Decker considered this information with his lips pursed, perhaps in irritation at the guards' laxness.

'And why are you here?'

Nathan stepped down from the step then gestured to Jeff for him to start his speech.

Jeff put on a wide smile.

'You know,' he said, drawling his words, 'this fort is a mighty fine testament to your administration, and I must say we're pleased we came.'

'It's good to hear that, but why—'

'And you know,' Jeff said, cutting Decker off with his louder voice, 'we can't help but wonder . . .' Jeff continued rambling on about nothing in particular, but he did walk towards the mayor's office.

Decker tried to interrupt the non-stop flow of words again and ask him what he wanted, but Jeff continued walking and talking.

Nathan had heard Jeff's rambling performance several times today and he couldn't help but smile as he followed him. Jeff was still talking when they reached the office, where the three men stood in the doorway.

As Decker was still staring at Jeff and trying to stop him talking with increasingly desperate gestures and louder interruptions, Nathan looked around the office.

Windows were at both ends of the square room, a cabinet stood against the wall on Nathan's side, and a desk was squarely in the middle of the room. These were the only items of furniture and although both were sturdy, neither was a suitable candidate for accepting the key.

Nathan caught Jeff's eye and winked, so Jeff mentioned that they were looking for work. Then he fell silent.

Decker continued to stare at Jeff, the irritated grinding of his teeth suggesting that he expected him to start talking again, then he shook his head.

'I wish you'd have just mentioned that straight away,' he snapped, then flashed a smile. When he spoke again his tone was calmer and more politic. 'I have no work for you. I barely have enough to occupy myself.'

Jeff shuffled his hulking form from foot to foot, his furrowed brow feigning disappointment, and after thanking Decker both men headed away to the steps where they stopped and looked back.

Decker had walked away from the doorway but he hadn't closed the door and Nathan edged to the side to get a different angle. From there he saw a shadow on the wall then that shadow lowered as Decker sat. A chair scraped, followed by silence.

Nathan and Jeff looked at each other, shrugged, then turned, but whereas Jeff headed to the steps leading down, Nathan turned to the other steps.

'We can't go up to the tower,' Jeff whispered. 'Decker has seen us.'

Nathan winked. 'We're looking for work and the tower is the best place to see the whole fort and town and what might be available.'

'That's a weak excuse and you know it.'

'It is, and we'll just have to keep to that story if he catches us. Now, be quiet and come on. We'll never find out where this money is if we don't take some risks.'

Nathan glanced back to confirm that Decker was still in his office. When he turned back Jeff had taken his advice and was hurrying up the steps. Nathan ran to catch up with him, placing his feet to the steps with as much care as he could while still hurrying out of sight as fast as possible.

Both men slowed when they were out of view from the mayor's office, then walked up the last of the steps to reach the next storey. This proved to open out on to the flat roof of the room below. Beyond that roof was the top of the wall around the plaza, the wall being wide enough for a man to walk along. This wall led to the wider walls of the outside of the fort.

Beside them was the squat and solid block of the tower with a short flight of steps inset into the walls, leading to a door. Joined to its side was a single building. This was less than half the height of the tower and it had a large, closed door with a solid lock.

Nathan and Jeff looked at each other, smiling. Nathan withdrew the key from his pocket and raised it high. Then, with mock stealth, he paced to the door with the key held out in his outstretched hand. He aligned it to the lock and pushed. The key entered the hole smoothly, but when he turned it, there was clear space on either side and the key turned impotently.

Nathan sighed and slapped the door in irritation, but to his surprise the door swung open and in the darkened interior, boxes and caskets were stacked high. Even before his eyes became accustomed to the gloom, he saw that many of them had locks, and that all of these locks were the right size to accept the key.

Nathan couldn't help but rub his hands with anticipation.

'Which one shall we try first?' he asked.

Jeff raised a hand, calling for him to be quiet, then darted his head to the side to glance at the steps leading down to the mayor's office.

'People,' he mouthed, cupping his ear.

A moment later Nathan heard the steady clump of footfalls, and he judged that two men were coming up the steps. He peered down into the open well of the steps to see that the men's shadows were on the wall and closing.

While they silently debated with raised eyebrows and pointing fingers whether the storeroom was the best place to hide, Nathan heard the approaching men murmur to each other, their words short instructions interrupted by bangs and thuds, then grunted curses.

Nathan made an instant assessment of who the men were and what they were doing. He grabbed Jeff's arm, then hurried to the steps leading into the tower. There were six inset steps before the door, giving them enough room to hide. They pressed themselves to the wall and listened.

More grunting, cursing and the occasional thud and scrape sounded before the men climbed out on to the roof then headed to the storeroom.

When their scraping footsteps had passed the tower, Nathan glanced out to confirm that his guess had been right. The two men were the guards and they were manoeuvring a casket, which the wagon had presumably delivered. The casket was wide enough almost to fill the stairwell and so the task of carrying it had been an onerous one. He darted back and whispered the details of what he'd seen to Jeff, who returned a hopeful grin.

With more raised eyebrows and pointing, they decided that once the guards had left they would check out the caskets in the storeroom. But they didn't get the chance. A creaking of the door above them heralded the worst possible turn of events. Somebody was in the tower.

The door at the top of the steps swung open and Nathan saw a hand emerge to grip the side of the door, but the person wasn't looking at them.

'I'll bring your food later,' the man said, then laughed.

Nathan didn't wait to hear the response as, with Jeff, he hurried over to the steps to the mayor's office and pattered down them. As they disappeared below the level of the roof, Nathan glanced to the side. The guards were still in the storeroom, but as they rounded the steps, Nathan heard the steady clump of footsteps as the man followed them down. He heard the guards call out to him, but he didn't hear their words as he and Jeff concentrated on escaping before they could be seen.

They speeded their descent, hurrying on to the first storey, noting that Decker was still in his office, then continued on to ground level. By the time they reached the plaza, both men were bounding with long strides. Jeff was in the lead and he looked back at Nathan, his mouth opening to say something, but he didn't get the chance to speak.

A man stepped out in front of him, his head down as he aimed to walk up the steps. They collided. Both men went down heavily, sprawling over each other.

'What the. . . ?' the man said before Jeff's substantial weight blasted the air from his lungs. They lay on the ground, entangled, until with a mixture of Jeff rolling away and the man kicking him away, they parted.

'Sorry about that,' Jeff said, rolling to his knees. He batted the dust from his legs and looked at Nathan for support, but Nathan stayed quiet. He'd seen the star on the fallen man's jacket – Jeff had knocked over Sheriff Buckthorn.

'Assaulting a lawman is a serious offence,' the podgy and grey-haired Buckthorn said, his small eyes flaring as he rubbed one of the rolls of fat around his belly.

Jeff spread his hands. 'It was an accident. I'm sorry.'

Buckthorn firmed his drooping jowls at first, but when he'd staggered to his feet and regained his breath with a few wheezing coughs, some of the belligerence had gone from his eyes. He looked over Nathan's shoulder at the steps and nodded towards them.

'That's as maybe, but you got no reason to be up there.'

'We were looking for work,' Nathan said, speaking quickly so they could get away before the man from the tower reached the plaza. 'And we reckoned—'

'I don't care what you reckoned. Everybody should stay out of there.'

'We know that now. We saw the mayor. He told us he had no work, so we left.' Nathan shrugged. 'You can ask him if you want.'

Buckthorn nodded. 'And I'll do just that.'

Nathan watched the direction of Buckthorn's gaze and realized he was looking at someone behind him. He turned to find that Mayor Decker had come down the steps and was considering them. The man from the tower was at his shoulder and was glaring at them.

'Their story is quite correct,' Decker said. 'They came up to see me, asking about work. I said there wasn't any, so they left.'

Buckthorn nodded and held a hand to the side, signifying they could go.

'Obliged,' Jeff and Nathan said together, then turned to go, but Decker tapped a foot on the bottom step, drawing their attention back to him.

'The trouble is,' he said, 'that was at least five minutes ago and I wonder why it took you all that time for you to come down from my office.'

Buckthorn snorted a harsh chuckle and swung round to glare at them.

'And now,' he said, 'I'm wondering that, too.'

He advanced on them but Mayor Decker raised a hand, halting him.

'You can do that wondering soon enough.' He clicked his fingers and the guard from the tower stepped out from behind him, drawing his gun.

Nathan and Jeff had left their guns in their saddle-bags and they had no choice but to raise their hands. To Decker's orders, they stood by the wall. Nathan couldn't help but notice that Decker directed them to stand before a spot where bullet holes riddled the wall. In a fort that had seen lengthy service this wasn't unexpected, but the brown stains around several of the holes looked worryingly recent.

Presently the other guards came down from the storeroom. Decker merely glanced at them, silently conveying an order which, from the way the guards rolled their shoulders, Nathan easily deduced. They paced up to them and without preamble, thundered blows into their guts which had them bending double. The next flurry of blows stood them upright and slammed them back against the wall.

With a gun on them, neither man dared to defend himself and they had no choice but to grit their teeth and endure. Throughout their beating Mayor Decker stood back, watching, as did Sheriff Buckthorn. Blow after blow rained down on them as the guards took the opportunity to pummel them. Punches landed on chests and faces, and neither guard appeared to be weakening. Every time they knocked them to the ground, they stood them up then knocked them down again.

Nathan reckoned he must have blacked out because suddenly he realized the blows had stopped. He opened his eyes to find he was lying curled up on the ground. Jeff was kneeling beside him with a hand on his shoulder.

'You fine?' he whispered.

Nathan provided a non-committal grunt then looked up to see that his resilient and large friend was managing to smile in defiance of a beating that despite his size and strength must still have hurt. Then he swung round to face Mayor Decker.

'That was just a warning,' Decker said, speaking slowly with grim authority. 'Now I'll hand you over to Sheriff Buckthorn. After he's dealt with you, if I ever see you again . . .'

Decker flicked his eyes to the side to look at the bullet-ridden wall. Nathan followed his gaze and this time, he had no doubt that the brown stains around the bullet holes were recent.

*

'And that's all we've got to say,' Nathan said.

'So,' Sheriff Buckthorn said, 'your story is that you were looking for work. You tried everywhere but didn't find any and then you tried the mayor's office, but he said no.'

'And so went up to the tower to see what was beyond the fort and where we could look for that work next.'

'A likely story.' Buckthorn shook his head then berated Nathan and Jeff with his contempt for them and his disbelief in Nathan's explanation of their actions.

After the beating the guards had inflicted on him, Nathan had no trouble in deafening his ears to mere complaints. He looked around the jailhouse. What he saw didn't fill him with hope.

The rest of the fort might have been in a state of crumbling disrepair, but the jailhouse wasn't. The walls were thick, the iron window-bars were well set and the huge door – which Nathan had noted was another likely recipient for the key – was formidable. And the row of cages along the back wall were each set away from the wall and had bars that were as close together and as thick as those in the windows.

Only one prisoner was within, sitting in the end cell on the floor. He was staring at his feet with his shoulders hunched and registering no interest in Buckthorn's stream of invective.

Nathan didn't mind the abuse. Compared to the beating it was a relief, and it took his mind off the key. Buckthorn had searched them and placed their belongings on the desk, including the key. He was sure that the sheriff would know it unlocked one of the caskets in the tower. Soon, he would surely confront them with an embarrassing fact they couldn't account for without raising plenty of other questions.

So Nathan tried to avoid looking at the key, but the strain of doing that was only drawing his gaze back to the rusty metal, sitting there in full view on the desk surrounded by coins.

'You can check out our story,' Jeff said, snapping Nathan out of his reverie.

'And I intend to,' Buckthorn grunted. Then he scooped up the key and coins and placed them in a box, which he pushed into a drawer. Then he directed them to the cages.

'Then why put us in there?' Jeff said, standing his ground.

Buckthorn shoved Jeff towards the cell. When he failed to move him an inch he backed away and glared at him, his hand darting to his holster.

'Quit complaining or I'll hand you back to Decker's guards.'

This time Jeff did as ordered and paced into the cell at the opposite end to the prisoner. Nathan joined him.

Buckthorn swung the cell door closed and locked it with a key from a large ring of similar keys. Nathan couldn't help but notice that they were all broadly of the same size as their key.

'And how long are we going to be in here?' Nathan asked.

'You'll stay in there,' Buckthorn said, 'until I prove you're innocent. And as you are, apparently, you got nothing to worry about.'

And with that taunt, Buckthorn returned to his desk,

placed the ring of keys on a hook on the wall behind his desk, then left the jailhouse, slamming and locking the heavy door behind him.

Nathan considered the prisoner, noting he was still sitting hunched and silent, then he shuffled closer to Jeff.

'He never even looked at our key,' he whispered.

'I know,' Jeff said, rubbing his ribs ruefully, 'and that just proves to me that the money is up in that store-room.'

Nathan narrowed his eyes. 'Why? What do you reckon is happening here?'

Jeff drew Nathan to the cell bars furthest away from the prisoner.

'I reckon Decker's been taking a cut of local trade or something similar and that cut gets delivered here, then taken up to the storeroom. Buckthorn is a straight lawman and knows nothing about it. And I reckon we've got every right to get our hands on Decker's ill-gotten dollars.'

Nathan smiled, noting that for all his hulking unsub-tle talk and actions, his friend had a quick mind, which he often failed to appreciate.

'Then we got to hope Buckthorn can prove our story.'

'He should. We asked for work everywhere. And even if he doesn't believe what he hears, we didn't do much of anything wrong.' Jeff kneaded his shoulders, winc-ing. 'That beating should be the worst we'll get.'

Nathan nodded. 'Yeah. Buckthorn can't keep us in here for more than a day or so. We should be out long before Wednesday.'

Jeff's questing fingers located a tender spot. His eyes

flared and in irritation he slapped a bar, the sound ringing in the jailhouse. Then he grabbed two bars and strained to pull them apart, his failed effort only confirming that there was no way out of the cell until the sheriff released them.

'We should,' he said, raising his voice for the first time, 'but I still hate being locked up and I sure don't want to spend a whole day in this place.'

Nathan was about to console Jeff, but a loud snort ripped out. He looked up to see the prisoner had raised his head and was looking at them.

'A whole day,' he intoned, his low voice hollow. 'You don't want to spend a *whole* day in this stinking rat-hole.'

'You can't blame us for that . . .' Nathan raised his eyebrows.

The prisoner looked aloft, shaking his head, then sneered.

'I'm Kenton Taylor. And I can blame you because some people just don't how lucky they are.'

Nathan guessed the reason for Kenton's sullen attitude and despite the urge to complain about his numerous aches and pains, he paced across the cell to be closer to him and ventured a smile.

'I guess it doesn't sound grateful from where you're sitting. How long have you been in here?'

'A week.'

'And how much longer have you got?'

'Five days,' Kenton grunted, then slapped the floor beside him.

'That ain't too bad.' Nathan raised his eyebrows, hoping for a less irritated response.

'It is, because on that day they'll drag me out of this

34

cell, take me into the plaza, and shoot me.' Kenton sighed then gestured across his chest, Nathan taking his action as his forming the sign of the cross.

Nathan gulped, backing a pace without thinking.

'What did you do?'

'They say I'm the man who shot Frank Reed.'

'And are you?'

'They say I am. So I'll die. What more is there to it than that?'

Nathan could think of nothing to say to this and lowered his head, but Jeff tapped his arm and drew him closer.

'Five days from now is Wednesday,' he whispered then raised his eyebrows. 'He dies on Wednesday.'

'So?'

Jeff tapped a huge finger against his temple.

'Remember what that dying man told us this morning.'

Nathan gave a slow nod, then drew Jeff into a conspiratory huddle.

'You're right,' he said. 'Maybe we got it wrong about the money being in the storeroom. Maybe we have to free him to get the money as a reward.'

'Or maybe not. Remember the initials on the gun the man gave us – *FR*. Frank Reed?' Jeff stared at Nathan until he winced. 'Perhaps we don't have to free him. Perhaps we have to use Frank's gun to kill him to get that ten thousand dollars reward.'

CHAPTER 3

'Who's Frank Reed?' Nathan asked, looking across the jailhouse at Kenton.

'Why do you want to know?' Kenton asked.

'Just making conversation.' Nathan shrugged. 'We could be sharing each other's company for a while.'

'Only until Wednesday.' Kenton snorted a harsh laugh. 'I ain't going to be too talkative after that. But you two are mighty talkative now, what with all that whispering about me.'

Nathan tipped back his hat as he considered his answer.

'Sorry about that. We were just debating whether we should talk to the man who they say shot Frank Reed.'

Kenton glared at them, then gave a slow shake of his head.

'Don't waste your breath.' Kenton shuffled round to place his back to them. 'I ain't exactly minded to talk.'

'Is there no chance of a reprieve?'

'They say I'm guilty and I should die. That ended it.' Kenton hunched his shoulders and drew his legs up to his chest. 'Now, I'm just waiting to die – in peace.'

Nathan nodded and in respect for Kenton's desire

for quiet turned away, but Jeff spoke up.

'What about friends?' he asked. 'Perhaps there's somebody out there trying to free you.'

Nathan glared at Jeff, his wide eyes chiding him for his unsubtle question as Kenton leapt to his feet and swirled round to face them.

'What you heard?' he demanded, standing before the bars.

'Nothing,' Jeff said, backing away a pace and raising his hands.

Kenton thrust an arm through the bars and aimed a shaking finger at him.

'Then don't go saying things like that and get a dying man's hopes up.' Kenton withdrew his hand then slapped the bars. He swung round to face away from them with a determined swing of the head and when he spoke again, his voice was low and defeated. 'Don't ever say things like that.'

Nathan stared at Jeff, shaking his head and urging him with his flared eyes to avoid upsetting him any more, but Jeff didn't look at him.

'Well, if you haven't got no friends out there,' he said, at least putting some compassion into his low tone, 'do you reckon there might be a friend of Frank Reed who wants to get his revenge on—'

'Jeff,' Nathan urged, pulling him back. 'You heard what he said. He doesn't want to talk about it.'

Jeff glared at him, his firm jaw suggesting he still had plenty of questions he wanted to ask, but he took Nathan's advice and quietened.

After that, none of them invited conversation again and after two hours of silent sitting, punctuated by the occasional groan when either man moved and found a new sore spot, the reek of whiskey heralded Sheriff Buckthorn's return. He clutched hold of the jailhouse door as if it were the only thing that was stopping him from falling, confirming that he had checked out their story while propping up the saloon bar.

'I got me some good news,' he said, his tone bright. He snaked across the jailhouse towards his desk, his grin showing none of the mistrust he'd shown before. 'Plenty of people agreed with your story.'

'That mean we can go?' Nathan asked.

Buckthorn swiped the keys from the hook, knocking them to the floor. He planted his feet wide and stooped over them, tutting as if the keys had made the mistake in not staying in his hand, then swooped down to pick them up.

'It sure does.' He clamped a tongue between his lips as he paced across the jailhouse, selecting the right key. 'I don't keep nobody in a cell who's looking for work.'

Buckthorn lunged for the lock, slipping the key in on his first attempt, and grinned at his success. He swung the door open. Both Nathan and Jeff released a sigh of relief.

'Obliged.'

Buckthorn waggled a finger at them. 'But take some advice, look for that work somewhere else. You annoyed Mayor Decker and if he sees you around, you won't live long enough to regret it.'

Buckthorn patted his substantial belly, then lurched round on the spot and staggered back to his desk. He placed the tin containing their belongings on his desk, then flopped into his chair and leaned back, pulling his hat down over his face.

Nathan followed him and pocketed the coins. He

avoided taking the key first but when he did, he slipped it in his pocket quickly.

'Don't worry,' Nathan said. 'We'll leave just as soon as we can.'

Without raising his hat, Buckthorn waved towards the door that led out on to the parade-ground, using a shooing-away gesture. Nathan followed Jeff from the jailhouse. But he stopped by the door to look at Kenton, who throughout their release hadn't looked up to acknowledge them. Then he considered the lock, noting that the keyhole was huge and larger than the key he had. The door that led into the plaza was the same size.

He headed outside. As the last rays of the dying sun were now reddening the tower, more people were wandering about and the guards were no longer outside the door to the tower. However, a glow lit the tunnel leading to the plaza and some chatter sounded, suggesting they were now sheltering inside and enjoying a smoke.

Nathan joined Jeff in slowly walking across the parade-ground, broadly heading towards the saloon.

'So,' he said, 'are we taking Buckthorn's advice?'

'The likes of Mayor Decker can't order me about,' Jeff said, jutting his chin defiantly, then he looked around. 'But this place ain't big enough for us to stay out of his way for long. If we're defying him, we got to be careful.'

Nathan nodded. 'Agreed. And either we got it right the first time and the key will get us in to one of those caskets in the storeroom, or the key is to Kenton Taylor's cell.'

'It could be a key to his cell, but to get the money, are

we supposed to free him or kill him?'

'You heard what Kenton said. They only *say* he killed Frank Reed. I reckon he's an innocent man and we have to free him.'

'All outlaws claim they're innocent, but whatever the answer, we got a bigger problem.' Jeff stopped midway across the parade-ground. 'Kenton is a convicted outlaw and even if I ain't following Decker's orders, I say we got no right getting involved with him.'

Nathan's initial reaction was to agree that they should just walk away, but the mystery of what they had to do here, and the possible reward of $10,000 if they worked it out, still intrigued him.

'I don't reckon anyone would have bothered trying to kill a man who'll die in five days. I reckon it's more likely we're supposed to free him.'

Jeff shook his head. 'And if we do that, Kenton could just slit our throats in the night and make off with everything we have.'

'He could, but he could also be innocent and we have at least to ask around before we leave.'

Jeff stomped round on the spot, sighing, his gaze taking in the jailhouse and the tower, before he turned back and provided a slow nod.

'Then I guess we'd better start by doing what Sheriff Buckthorn did and ask about Kenton in the saloon.'

Nathan readily agreed to this plan with a huge grin. Two minutes later they were leaning on the bar in the saloon. Two men wearing the red coats that identified them as being Decker's men were amongst the customers. As neither of them was one of the guards who'd beaten them, Nathan subtly questioned the bartender under the guise of finding out with whom they'd just shared the jailhouse.

'Kenton Taylor and Frank Reed,' the bartender said, then gave a low whistle. 'Now there is one sorry tale.'

Nathan and Jeff leaned closer.

'Go on,' Jeff urged.

'Kenton and Frank are the only surviving sons of two warring ranchers to the south of Providence. The Bar J and Bar Z range war ripped everyone apart for some ten years, but both families lost so many kin that they reached a truce five years back.'

'But now that truce's ended?' Nathan asked.

The bartender shrugged. 'Frank's death was the first thing I'd heard of to suggest that it had. After their fathers died, Kenton's sister, Nancy, married Frank Reed and their cattle have carried a new brand, the Bar T.'

Jeff nodded towards a spare table, his downcast eyes suggesting he'd heard enough to convince him they'd be wrong to get involved in this, but Nathan was reluctant to relent just yet.

'Who'll run the Bar T when both Frank and Kenton are out of the way?'

'Could be Nancy, but the rumour I'd heard . . .' The bartender glanced around, confirming nobody was close. 'Mayor Decker has been buying up land at rock-bottom prices and his territory now reaches from here to the Bar T. The rumour is that once Kenton pays for what he did, Decker will buy up the ranch for another low price.'

Nathan detected the suspicion in the bartender's low tone and he reckoned he'd have said more if one of the red-coated men hadn't then come to the bar.

'I'd heard about you two,' he said, standing up to

Nathan and Jeff and glaring at them in turn. 'Enjoy this one drink, then leave town.'

The man turned on his heel without building on his threat, and headed back to his table. While the bartender poured them two whiskeys Nathan glanced at Jeff and, despite the threat, Nathan saw the renewed interest in his lively eyes.

'You reckon there's anything suspicious about that rumour?' Nathan asked the bartender.

'Nope,' the bartender said in a loud voice, his darting eyes and nervous polishing of the bar replacing his previous enthusiasm for idle chatter. He pushed their drinks towards them.

'But you sounded suspicious.'

'Sure didn't,' the bartender said, then lowered his voice and leaned towards Nathan, his eyes wide and darting. 'As you didn't understand your warning – people who ignore advice or talk too much . . . Let's just say nobody gets to see them again.'

Nathan decided not to push him with any more questions as the warning from Decker's man had clearly spooked him. He turned away, but then turned back and asked one final question.

'Where did Kenton kill Frank?'

'Out at the Bar T,' the bartender said, shrugging. 'Mayor Decker was the only witness and he saw him blast Frank right between the eyes. Now, you've asked too many questions and if I were you, I'd shut up and go.'

The bartender hurried off down the bar to deal with another customer, leaving Nathan and Jeff to head to a table near the door.

'All right,' Jeff said, when he'd checked that nobody

was close enough to hear. 'I agree the case against Kenton sounds mighty suspect and we ought to consider breaking him out. But we're in a fort under Decker's control and we've been told to leave. How can we hope to break a man out of such a solid jailhouse before someone gives us more than just another warning?'

'A jailhouse ain't as strong as the bars on the windows and the thickness of the walls. It's as strong as the person defending it. So we can use the subtle way.' Nathan pointed to the bar. 'Buckthorn reeked of whiskey and I reckon he's wishing he could check out our story some more in here.'

Jeff snorted. 'So you reckon one of us should just invite him here for a drink while the other frees Kenton?'

'Nope.' Nathan stood and turned to the door. 'We'll do the next best thing.'

'What you two want now?' Buckthorn muttered, pacing back from the door. 'I told you to leave town.'

Nathan glanced across the parade-ground to confirm that nobody had followed them out of the saloon, then headed into the jailhouse with Jeff at his side.

'We want to ask you where we should go next.'

Buckthorn shuffled round to face them. 'Don't care. Decker's got his eyes on you. I reckon you should just go somewhere where Decker ain't.'

'I didn't mean that. You hear things.' Nathan noted Buckthorn was still sneering, so he withdrew the whiskey bottle from his pocket. 'Perhaps you'd like to tell us what you've heard recently.'

Buckthorn's eyes lit up and his hand reached for the bottle before he tore his gaze away from it and lowered his hand.

'About what?'

Nathan shrugged. 'About things you've heard, people who've passed through who've hired before, comings and goings. We might then get us an idea about where to go.'

Buckthorn rubbed his jaw, then lowered and shook his head.

'I don't know much about all of that.'

'A pity.' Nathan slotted the bottle back in his pocket and turned to the door.

'But it won't hurt to talk,' Buckthorn shouted after him. 'Perhaps I might remember something you can use when I've had a drink inside me – it loosens the mind.'

Nathan turned back and nodded. He sat on the edge of Buckthorn's desk while Buckthorn fetched three mugs and poured generous measures for them.

Nathan took the lead in questioning Buckthorn to avoid Jeff asking any unsubtle questions, but Buckthorn was in a talkative mood and didn't appear to view their presence as being sinister. So he soon relented and let Jeff take over directing Buckthorn's chatter.

Jeff kept to the safe subjects of where they might find work and who might hire them and this encouraged Buckthorn to ramble on between swigging the whiskey. Everything he said rapidly veered back to his mistrust of Decker and he related a catalogue of complaints about his actions since he'd taken over two years ago. He confirmed his success in buying up the land around Fort Benton and he commented on how local traders often sent him goods for little or no charge.

Throughout his complaints, Nathan and Jeff sipped their drinks, the liquor helping to dull their aches, but they refused a refill at least three times as many times as they accepted. Even then they both surreptitiously spilled whiskey on the floor when Buckthorn wasn't looking their way.

Early on, Nathan caught Kenton's eye in the end cell. From his bright eyes and attentive posture Nathan reckoned he was wise to what they were trying to do. But when Kenton swayed from side to side, miming being the inebriated sheriff, then drew a finger across his neck, Nathan turned his back on him and rejoined the chatter.

Several hours later, the second bottle was almost empty and Nathan was wondering whether they'd have to risk heading to the saloon to buy another when Buckthorn started to suffer from his excesses. First, his eyes glazed. Then they closed. His head lowered until his chin rested on his chest.

Jeff glanced at Nathan then nudged the sheriff. This brought him sufficiently awake to refill his mug. He brought it to his lips, leaning back in his chair, then continued leaning back and back until the chair toppled. He landed flat on his back with him still lying with legs elevated and splayed over the front of the chair.

As the whiskey pooled out of the mug, a loud snore rasped out. Jeff nudged him with a toe, this time receiving another snore.

'He's definitely passed out,' Jeff said.

'Then hurry up,' Kenton said from his cell, 'and get me out of here.'

'Be quiet,' Nathan said, kneeling beside Jeff and watching the sleeping sheriff to confirm he wouldn't suddenly open an eye and demand yet another refill.

'We don't want to wake him. He's only drunk.'

'Then knock him out like I tried to—'

'We ain't doing that,' Nathan snapped, waving his hands downwards in a sign that Kenton should keep his voice down. 'We want to be able to explain ourselves if this all goes wrong.'

Kenton looked skyward a moment. 'Then quit talking and get me out of this cell and nothing *will* go wrong.'

Nathan stood, extending his legs slowly. He patted Jeff's back then bade him to stand by the door to the parade-ground and check nobody was approaching the jailhouse. Then he paced around the sheriff and over to the cell, walking quietly and slipping the key from his pocket. He slotted the key in the lock.

It'd been some hours since he'd convinced himself that the key would fit Kenton's cell. So his discovery that the key was too large for the lock shocked him. He flinched back, then shrugged and tried the key again. It still didn't fit.

'The keys are over there,' Kenton said, pointing to the hook behind Buckthorn's desk.

Nathan stared at the key in his hand, his mind whirling. As the key didn't fit the lock to Kenton's cell, there was now no reason to suppose they had to free Kenton to get the $10,000 reward. The fact that he would get shot on Wednesday was probably just a coincidence, after all.

'It's all quiet out there,' Jeff said from the door. 'And I can't see those guards. Hurry up and get him out.'

'But the key,' Nathan intoned. 'It doesn't fit.'

Kenton glared at him through the bars as Nathan fingered the key, his shock rooting him to the spot. Jeff again urged him to be quick, then hurried over to the desk and collected the loop of keys. He glanced at Nathan as he passed him, then fumbled through the keys to find one of the right size, his raised eyebrows questioning him as to what was wrong.

Nathan was still pondering on whether, after discovering that the key didn't fit the lock, there was any real evidence to support his theory that the men in the gunfight were planning to break Kenton out of jail.

He had just decided there wasn't and, even more important, even if there was, he shouldn't have used that as a reason to break even a dubiously convicted murderer out of jail when Kenton lunged through the bars.

Nathan saw his intent and also lunged, but he was too late and Kenton snatched the loop from Jeff's grasp. With a deft twirl of the wrist, he found the right key. His quick actions spoke of the time he'd spent in an apparent stupor when he was in fact noting any possible ways to escape if an opportunity arose.

He bent his wrist round to fit the key in the lock and with a quick flick sprung the lock and pushed open the cell door. Nathan winced and moved to push the door closed, but Kenton had already kicked it fully open and was hurrying past him to the door. He glanced back at them, beckoning them to follow. With no choice, Nathan hurried after him.

Kenton slipped out of the jailhouse and stood beside the door. He glanced left and right, then nodded and edged to the side to let Nathan and Jeff follow him out.

Jeff slowly closed the door behind them while Nathan joined Kenton in looking around. The night was still. The only noise came from the saloon across the parade-ground and nobody else was visible. Even the tower appeared to be unguarded.

'This,' Nathan said, 'might be a good time to talk about—'

Kenton slapped a hand over his mouth, silencing him.

'Like you said to me, be quiet,' he urged. Kenton kept Nathan's mouth covered for several seconds then raised his hand. 'Now, we have to get away. Where's your horses?'

Nathan winced as he felt another twinge of concern, but he had to acknowledge the sense of their getting away quickly.

He pointed. 'The stables.'

Kenton nodded. Keeping to the shadows, he hurried along beside the jailhouse wall, then scurried across to the stables. Nathan and Jeff waited until he'd found the shadows, then, one at a time, ran after him.

When Nathan had joined Kenton he ran his gaze over the jailhouse, the mayor's office and the tower, but saw no sign that anyone was looking their way from the gaunt and dark buildings. The parade-ground was still deserted and the gates were open.

When Jeff joined them they hurried along in the shadows and slipped into the stables, heading to the far end to a stall nearest the main gates.

'Only two horses?' Kenton asked when they reached their horses.

'Yeah,' Nathan said. 'I'll take that horse. You can ride doubled-up with Jeff.'

As Jeff grunted and started to ask why he had to be the one who rode doubled-up, Kenton shook his head then pointed at the horses in the stalls around them.

'Forget that. We'll just take another horse.'

He moved towards the next stall, but Nathan grabbed his arm, halting him.

'We don't steal.'

'But you do break men out of jail, and that's far too serious a crime to be worrying about committing another crime right now.' Kenton looked at Nathan's hand until Nathan raised it, then swung round to face him and set his hands on his hips. 'You got a gun?'

Nathan's mouth went dry. He delivered a worried glance at Jeff, who returned that glance, then darted his gaze between Nathan and Kenton.

Nathan faced up to Kenton and shook his head.

'We broke you out of jail and that means we say how this escape goes. And we won't use a gun, just like we won't steal a horse.'

Kenton met Nathan's gaze, receiving a steely glare in return, then looked at Jeff to see him back up Nathan's comment with a flexing of his large fists. He lowered his head and when he spoke again, his voice was softer.

'All right. Like you say, you're in charge and if you don't want to steal or use no gun, that's what we'll do.' Kenton looked up and patted Nathan's shoulder, the action cheering Nathan for the first time since they'd freed him. 'But we might face some trouble on the way out and then we'll need a few warning shots to escape. So what do you say?'

Nathan considered the more compliant Kenton, then returned a nod.

'I guess you're right. We both got a gun.' Nathan pointed at his saddle-bag. 'But like I say we—'

Kenton barged past him and headed to Nathan's horse. He rummaged in the bag, emerging with Nathan's gun, leaving the initialled Peacemaker inside.

He thumbed back the six-shooter's hammer then placed the chamber to his ear and whirled it, nodding. Then, with a few deft twitches of the wrist, he loaded the gun.

'Any other guns?'

'Unless things get mighty desperate, Jeff's will stay in his saddle-bag.'

A momentary smile crossed Kenton's features, sending another twinge of concern rippling through Nathan's stomach.

Kenton hefted the six-shooter, the metal catching a stray beam of light through the open stable door.

'Got anything else worth taking?' he grunted.

'Taking?' Nathan said.

As Kenton sniggered, Jeff snorted and glared at him.

'I'll tell you one thing for sure,' he said, pointing at him, 'we won't take you with us if you don't start acting a whole heap more grateful.'

Jeff rolled his shoulders and looked to Nathan for support, but Nathan had seen the intent behind Kenton's question.

He took a long pace towards Kenton, but that only encouraged Kenton to swing the gun round to aim it at his stomach.

'A pity,' Kenton said. 'Then I'll just have to take your horses and see what I can get for them.'

With no choice, Nathan raised his hands and backed away a pace.

'You ungrateful snake,' he grunted.

'Yeah,' Jeff said from beside him while raising his hands. 'We broke you out of jail and you're repaying us by robbing us.'

Kenton shrugged. 'Just think yourself lucky I'm not going to slit your throats.'

CHAPTER 4

'I can't believe he did that,' Nathan said from the stable door as he watched Kenton gallop through the gates, leaving them stranded in the fort.

'I can,' Jeff grumbled, then glanced into the stables. 'But I'm not stealing someone's horse, no matter how much trouble we're in. So I reckon we got no choice but to get out of the fort and find somewhere to hide before the sun comes up.'

Nathan acknowledged Jeff's honesty in this desperate situation with a firm pat on the back. Then they slipped away from the stables and, keeping beside the fort wall, headed over to the gates. They were ten paces away from the heavy open gates when a voice tore out from the jailhouse.

'Kenton Taylor's escaped,' Sheriff Buckthorn cried out, hanging on to the jailhouse door. He pushed himself away from the door, swayed, then staggered out into the parade-ground, snaking his way towards the saloon. 'He's gone. They've all gone!'

Nathan and Jeff slid to a halt. If they headed through the gates, Buckthorn would be sure to see them, so they slipped back to press themselves to the fort wall and hide in the darkest shadows. They were rewarded for their caution when Buckthorn stomped to a halt in the middle of the parade-ground and swung round to look towards the gates, then pointed.

'And they're getting away,' he shouted. 'I can still see them.'

As he hurried on to the saloon, calling out for help, Nathan and Jeff had just seconds to decide whether they should risk running through the gates. They decided that if Buckthorn was intent on raising a posse to chase after Kenton, they should stay here.

Nathan drew Jeff to follow him along the wall. The gates were thrown wide open and there was a gap between the gate and the wall of several feet, which they slipped into.

The gate was solid enough to ensure that nobody would be able to see them hiding there even in daylight. Through a thin gap between two planks, they watched an inebriated gaggle of men spill out of the saloon, then hurry over to stand before the gates and peer into the darkness.

Within minutes, Buckthorn had gathered together sufficient people to chase after Kenton. These men's enthusiasm was liquor fuelled and their raucous shouting confirmed that they reckoned a chase was a good way to end the evening.

But a small group of red-coated men emerged with Mayor Decker and these men stayed away from the rabble. Amongst them, Nathan recognized the two guards who had beaten them in the plaza. Decker's men huddled and watched the group led by the inebriated sheriff mount up, then hurtle off into the night with much whooping and hollering that was sure to warn Kenton of their pursuit.

Then they looked to Decker for instruction. He, with authoritative pointing in various directions and some low orders that Nathan couldn't hear, organized them for leaving the fort. When they rode out through the gates, these men used a measured and orderly pace.

The customers from the saloon who hadn't chased after Kenton milled around the parade-ground for a while. Some headed to the gates and squinted into the darkness while wagering on whether or not Kenton would get away, and, if not, which group would catch him. But when the whooping from the sheriff's group had faded into the distance, they accepted they wouldn't be able to see what was happening in the dark and returned to the saloon.

'And what now?' Jeff asked when the parade-ground had returned to quiet and stillness.

'We know which way Kenton and everyone else went. I reckon we go the other way.'

Jeff snorted a laugh. 'Now for the first time today, that's one of your plans I don't mind hearing.'

They slipped out from behind the gate. As Jeff took a last look around the fort Nathan's gaze centred on the tower. It loomed over them with its dark form outlined against the cloudy night sky beyond. The windows were black holes and now that their misguided actions had proved that freeing Kenton wasn't connected with the $10,000, Nathan couldn't help but think about the possibility of the money being behind one of those windows.

'You know,' he mused, 'I reckon—'

'Stop reckoning and stop staring at that tower,' Jeff urged, tugging Nathan's arm. 'They won't be gone for ever.'

'But they will be gone for a while.' Nathan beckoned Jeff to join him in looking at the tower. 'And as we can never come back here, I reckon this is the last chance we'll ever get to find out whether we can use our key.'

'You're not still thinking of . . .' Jeff sighed, looking aloft.

'Sure am. You with me?'

Jeff shook his head and swung round to peer down at him.

'Won't you ever learn to ignore that curiosity of yours? We interfered in a gunfight and killed a man. We got ourselves beaten up. We got ourselves arrested. We got told to leave town or face a firing-squad. We broke an outlaw out of jail. And now we're wanted men and we're stranded in a fort.'

'Yeah, and more important than that is the fact we got nothing to show for it all. But now that Decker and Buckthorn have gone after Kenton, we've got enough time before we have to hightail it out of here to check out the storeroom.'

'We haven't.'

Nathan considered Jeff's belligerent stance, then reached up to pat his shoulder.

'Well, we won't have if we stand around talking about it all night.' Nathan turned to set off towards the stables. 'Come on. It'll only take a few minutes.'

Jeff still loitered by the gate, and for several paces Nathan thought he'd refuse to follow him, but when he kept going Jeff sighed and hurried after him.

Nathan suppressed a smile as his friend again acquiesced to his plans. He resolved to keep quiet until the thought of the money had rekindled his enthusiasm.

Staying in the shadows, they circled around the edge

of the parade-ground to reach the stables, then slipped inside and hurried over to the other door to emerge opposite the tower. There, they looked up at the gaunt block, confirming there were no guards outside the door or any sign that anyone was inside. Then they hurried across to the tower where they pressed themselves against the wall, catching their breaths, before slipping in through the doorway.

They hurried through the tunnel to emerge into the plaza. The light-level here was so low they had to pace slowly along with Nathan leading and with Jeff resting a hand on his shoulder as he used his memory of the layout to reach the steps.

In the dark, Nathan and Jeff both stumbled on the first step, but when they'd confirmed their height, they pattered up them, rounding them on their circular path. With the only lights in the fort coming from the saloon, they were in almost complete darkness and they walked with their hands outstretched as they circled round.

Some light drifted into the space outside the mayor's office to light their way, but that again faded as they embarked on the climb up the second set of steps to reach the roof.

Their progress was easier when they emerged out on to the roof. Here they had the ambient light from the cloudy night sky and the low full moon even threatened to break through the clouds, giving them enough light to see the area beyond the fort. Nathan could see the settlement and the trail beyond on which Decker and Buckthorn would be chasing after Kenton, but he couldn't see any of the riders. And that meant they still had some time before they returned.

With a burst of anticipation lightening his step, Nathan headed to the storeroom where the door was still open. Jeff followed him in, ducking to avoid the low doorway. Then he stepped to the side and held the door wide open to provide him with some light.

The room wasn't as large as Nathan had remembered from his earlier brief visit, but a stack of five identical caskets stood by the far wall. The casket the men had brought up sat by the door.

Nathan paced across the room, then removed the key to try the topmost casket. The key stabbed against the lock and refused to enter no matter how hard he pressed. When he stood to the side to avoid his shadow lying over the lock, he confirmed that the key was too large.

A glance at the other caskets confirmed that they all had identical locks, but he still tried them, without success.

With each failure Jeff grumbled. When the last casket failed to open he kicked the casket by the door, but his action rocked the lid up before it crashed back down.

In the darkened room, each man looked at the other, grinning. Then Jeff dropped to his knees and threw back the lid. He snorted, then rocked back on his haunches to let Nathan see inside. No money was in there, just rows of rifles, the polished wood glistening in the faint light.

'No money, just guns,' Jeff murmured.

'Or perhaps Decker's turned the money into guns.'

Jeff considered the caskets. 'The bartender said local traders sell Decker goods for low prices or even give them to him. Perhaps those goods are in these caskets.'

'But what do they hope to get in return?'

'Perhaps they don't have much of a choice, like we don't now.' Jeff stood and laid a hand on Nathan's shoulder. 'Agreed?'

Nathan looked at the rifles, sighing, then closed the lid. He was about to agree with Jeff and leave, but a thought came to him. They had tried every place in the fort that might accept a large key, except one.

'Just give me one more minute and then we'll go.'

Jeff winced and looked aloft as Nathan slipped past him, beckoning him to follow, then heading to the steps to the tower. Nathan didn't expect that anyone would be inside, but he quietly paced up to the door, then peered through the barred inset window into the room beyond. It was deserted.

He fingered the door, searching for the lock, but the door was broken where the lock would once have been and the light pressure of his touch was enough to open the door. He stepped inside.

Aside from the straw strewn all over the floor, the room was bare. Two windows were on each of three walls. The fourth wall backed on to the storeroom and, in the place where the windows would have been, two grilles were set into the wall.

Unwilling to accept that his quest to use the key had now ended, Nathan stood before the nearest window. With his hands thrown up on either side of the window and his shoulders hunched, he cast his gaze around the fort. Slowly he searched for somewhere else to try before they left the fort and the mystery of the key and the money behind for ever.

'That minute's up,' Jeff said from the door. 'Now, we got to go.'

Nathan provided a reluctant nod and looked up to the sky, sighing. From behind thick clouds the moon emerged, bathing the fort in sudden harsh light and, realizing that he was standing in full view before the window, Nathan swung back to press himself to the wall.

'Yeah,' he said, 'but let the moon go away again before we sneak off.'

Jeff slipped away from the door and joined Nathan in standing against the wall, as the moon cast long rectangles of cold light across the room, confirming that it was empty.

'It's a pity we couldn't find out where we could use that key,' Jeff said, turning to Nathan. He sighed. 'But we really have tried everywhere. You know that, don't you?'

'Yeah,' Nathan murmured. He looked around the room, considering the windows and the different views they each provided of the fort.

'I said,' Jeff persisted, 'we really have tried everywhere and now we have to go and never ever return here. Agreed?'

Jeff continued to stare at Nathan as he ran his gaze around the room. They *had* tried everywhere in the fort and a key this large needed a large lock, but they'd found nowhere where they could use it. But neither had this tower or the storeroom been locked, and that suggested that they had failed to locate the right place to look.

On the other hand, Nathan now noticed several ground-in tobacco-stains on the floor amongst the straw and detected the stench of cigar smoke. So maybe this tower was normally guarded, but the occupant had left suddenly to join in the chase after Kenton and in so doing had provided them with this singular opportunity.

Nathan sighed, noting he'd probably never find out the truth and that this failure would haunt him long beyond the Wednesday deadline. But he continued to look and think, the pressing need to leave sharpening his mind and his senses as he ran through the possibilities.

Then his gaze fell on the grilles in the wall that backed onto the storeroom.

They were three feet square with five solid vertical bars. Behind the nearest he saw a few inches of the thick wall reflecting the moonlight, then nothing. He narrowed his eyes, deciding that the fact that he could see nothing wasn't because the light wasn't strong enough to intrude further. There was a large space behind the grille.

'But,' he mused, 'perhaps we haven't tried everywhere yet.'

Nathan lowered his head to pass by the window and shuffled over to the grille by the door, but just as he was reaching out to it, the moon slipped behind cloud again, plunging the tower into darkness.

'Whatever you want to do,' Jeff said, 'do it quick.'

In the dark, Nathan ran his fingers up and down the bars, then reached inside. A breeze cooled his hand, coming from behind the wall. Although he could see nothing ahead, the musty smell and coolness gave him the impression that there was a considerable space beyond the grille.

He reached up. Above the grille he felt nothing beyond the wall, and the same to the left and right. But when he felt downwards, his hand closed on a block of metal, and his questing fingers found a hole – a keyhole to a lock. He couldn't help but gasp.

'What is it?' Jeff asked.

Nathan kept a finger on the hole then removed the key and, using his finger as a guide, reached through the grille and slipped it in the lock. The key disappeared inside.

'Cross your fingers,' he said, looking up at Jeff. 'This could be it.'

Nathan turned the key and from beyond the grille, he heard a faint click.

'It worked!' Jeff said, kneeling down beside him, then he lowered his voice. 'It worked.'

'It sure did.'

Nathan removed the key then stood. He considered the grille, then pushed it, but it didn't move. He leaned back to open the door and give him more light with which to consider the grille. Then he gripped two bars and shoved and shoved.

Jeff rolled his substantial shoulders, then joined him. The two men strained hard as they pushed the grille, but it still didn't move. Then, with a bashful glance at each other, they stopped pushing and pulled. With a sudden lurch and a grinding of metal on metal, the grille swung upwards and away from the wall, revealing the darkened space beyond.

With Jeff patting his back, Nathan poked his head through the hole. He reckoned he was looking into a gap between the wall to the tower and the wall to the storeroom. Further along he saw the faint outline of light thrown through the second grille onto an interior wall. And the cool breeze running over his face was stronger now.

'What do you see?' Jeff asked.

'It's a space between the walls, but I can't see nothing without more light.'

'And we can't risk getting any. It'd be seen all over the fort.'

Nathan nudged his head out, then swung his legs back in and climbed into the space. He stayed crouched down as he peered out at Jeff.

'Agreed. But we have to find out what's in here now, don't we?'

'Yeah, but . . .' Jeff flinched back, his ear cocked high, then he crouched over and hurried to a window. He glanced up, then ducked down and returned to the grille. 'Riders are coming back to the fort.'

'Buckthorn or Decker?'

'I don't intend to stay long enough to find out. This *is* our only chance to find out what's behind there, but do that finding real quick.'

Nathan nodded, then turned, still crouched, and raised his hands above his head, confirming there was enough room for him to stand. He stood and splayed his hands wide, feeling ahead.

He had to act quickly, but walking in darkness was uncomfortable. He imagined a wall was just inches from his nose and with every faltering step, he dreaded slamming into it. But he shuffled ahead for two paces before his fingers touched a wall. Then he took three slow paces to the right before he reached the wall to the side and level with the door.

He swung round, placing his back to the wall, and looked ahead. The faint square of light from the other grille was ahead, but that only gave him a point of reference and not enough light to see what was within this enclosed space.

He shuffled his feet along the floor, questing in long sweeps ahead of him, but he only scraped across grit. He moved forward until he was level with the grille, then took another two sweeping paces.

Outside, Jeff murmured confirmation that Decker was leading the returning riders, but Nathan put that from his mind. He took another pace, then swept around with his feet.

Jeff again urged him to hurry and after taking another pace and again feeling nothing, Nathan accepted that unless the $10,000 was in an obvious place like a casket, he was unlikely to happen across it. Certainly if it was in a recess in the walls he stood no chance of finding it.

'How close is he?' Nathan asked, abandoning his cautious approach and taking a long stride forward.

'Decker and ten men are riding into the settlement. We ain't going to be able to slip away through the gates for a while now.'

'Don't worry. We'll find somewhere to hide.' Nathan considered. 'And let's hope he hasn't captured Kenton.'

'I can't see anyone with him who looks like a prisoner.' Jeff pattered over to the grille and peered in. 'But how will that help?'

'If he didn't find him, he'll think we got away too and won't see no reason to look out for us hiding right under his nose.'

Nathan took another stride then prodded forward, but his foot didn't scrape across grit this time and he toppled. He threw out his hands as he fell forward, his foot eventually landing on a solid surface, but by then he was on his knees and nursing a numb ankle.

'Don't make so much noise,' Jeff said. 'Decker's coming in through the gates.'

Nathan sat and rubbed his ankle. 'I'm trying not to. There's some steps in here and I just tried to throw myself down them.'

'Then throw yourself down them quickly, and quietly.'

Nathan felt around him, feeling the step below him and the one below that. The breeze on his face was rising, giving him the impression this gap between the walls carried on downwards for a while, perhaps to the storey below and the mayor's office. That meant he wouldn't have enough time to explore the whole space now.

With a resigned sigh, he stood and turned, seeing the outline of Jeff's face peering at him through the grille.

'I'm coming out,' he said. 'I reckon this space is huge.'

'All right,' Jeff said. 'But if we can find somewhere to hide, we can try again after Decker's gone to bed.'

'Glad you're getting curious now.' Nathan looked around him. 'What about hiding in here?'

Jeff joined him in peering around then shivered.

'Been a prisoner once before today and I didn't enjoy it. I ain't volunteering to hide in there.'

The faint image of Jeff's frowning face came into view as the light-level suddenly rose.

'Agreed,' Nathan said.

Jeff glanced over his shoulder, wincing.

'That moon is choosing the wrong moment to come out and I can hear Decker getting closer.' He backed away from the grille, then returned. 'He's outside the jailhouse now and he could come up here. Get out.'

Nathan nodded and moved to leave, but he also looked around, noting in the stronger light what he could see of the space for future reference. It was two paces wide and empty and the steps he was sitting on led down for around twenty steps to a level that he judged to be around fifteen feet higher than the mayor's office. Then the steps did an abrupt left turn and disappeared from view.

As he backed away to the grille, the moon again slipped behind cloud, lowering the light-level. Jeff stood back to give him enough room to climb out, and as he slipped a leg through the grille, from outside Nathan heard men talking, the sounds coming from below them at the base of the tower.

Jeff moved towards the door as the moon again flitted out from behind the clouds, illuminating the room. Jeff looked at him, wincing, and Nathan returned the wince, then used the light, which almost immediately faded again, to take a last look at the area behind the wall.

He looked down the steps, running his gaze down the walls and storing away the memory. His gaze reached the bottom step, and then Nathan flinched.

A man was standing at the bottom of the steps, looking up at him. He was thin and his clothes and face were dirt-streaked. His sunken eyes and bowed back told Nathan that this man wasn't one of Decker's men.

'What are you doing here?' Nathan blurted out, hearing his lame question echo back at him from the walls.

The man moved his head to the side as if he was about to shake it and his caloused hands rose, perhaps in a warding-off gesture. Then he darted away to disappear from view, his receding footfalls pattering away down more steps, the darkness closing in at the same time and almost making Nathan believe his sighting had been of an apparition.

'I'm waiting until I'm sure the moon won't come out again,' Jeff said from the door. 'Then we can get out of here.'

'I wasn't speaking to you,' Nathan said, raising his other leg to climb out through the grille. 'I saw someone down there.'

'You sure?' Jeff asked, swirling round to face him.

'Yeah.' Nathan slipped the grille back down into place, hearing the lock click as it locked. 'But I scared him and he ran off. I reckon he's Decker's prisoner.'

Jeff opened the door. 'I've heard that tone in your voice several times today. That mean you want to come back later and free him?'

Nathan considered, as from down below he heard voices closing and footsteps clattering through the tunnel. He didn't know whether Decker and his men would come up to the tower, but they couldn't risk that they would. And that meant they'd have to leave here and find somewhere to hide quickly.

'I hope so,' he said, raising his voice as much as he dared in the hope that the prisoner would hear him. He looked through the grille, imagining what it'd be like to live in that cold and inhospitable prison behind the walls.

He tore his gaze away to see Jeff nod, his firm jaw showing his approval of Nathan's decision. Then they slipped through the door and headed down on to the roof.

The moon was behind cloud, but in the parade-ground a glow illuminated the stables as the returned people held up lights. By that light Nathan saw several men leading horses into the stables, and he heard the footfalls of at least two men heading up the steps to the tower.

Then their voices carried up to Nathan.

'I'm telling you. I saw two men heading this way.'

'Just two?' Nathan was sure this reply came from Decker.

'Yeah. They came out of the stables and went across to the tower. I'm guessing Kenton got away, but the men who—'

'I don't want to hear your guess, just what you saw.'

'Then two men definitely headed up here.'

As they didn't have the time to head down the steps and seek refuge below, Nathan looked around, searching for a hiding-place. The roof had several blocks behind which they could hide, but not for long if Decker searched thoroughly. Aside from the tower, the only other potential hiding-place was the storeroom, and there was nowhere to hide in there. But beyond the storeroom, the wall led away on its circuit of the plaza until at its far end it joined the wall to the main fort.

If they headed along that wall, their forms would be silhouetted against the night sky, but they'd only be visible if someone was standing in the plaza or on the other side of the wall and looking up. And as the men who had returned were either taking their horses to the stables or coming up the steps, Nathan reckoned nobody was in a position to see them.

He patted Jeff's arm, then hurried past the store-room to the wall. Without discussion Jeff followed him.

Nathan ran as fast as he dared along the wall in the poor light, with Jeff at his heels. Over the pattering of his feet, he couldn't hear whether Decker was still talking, and with every pace he expected him to emerge on to the roof and shout out at them to stop. But he reached the main wall without challenge.

The wall stretched away on either side with enough space for them to walk together, and on the side of that wall there was a short wall behind which the fort defenders would once have stood. This wall was five feet high in parts, but had crumbled away for long stretches.

As Jeff reached the wall, he heard voices again. Then he saw a glow spread out along the roof before the steps, the forms and elongated shadows of three men emerging.

Nathan and Jeff were just fifty or so paces from the tower. If they were to run along the wall they would be clearly visible to these men. Even if they were to move slowly and crawl along the crumbled sections, Nathan judged his – and especially the large Jeff's – chances of being seen as high. But as the glow from the brands didn't reach them, they hunkered down before the short wall and looked towards the tower.

Decker emerged on to the roof, followed by two other men. They lined up, peering around. Their gazes ran over the tower, then the roof and walls until Nathan and Jeff were in their direct line of sight, but they continued turning until they'd completed a circle.

Nathan breathed a sigh of relief that they had been lucky. Standing before the dark wall, they would remain lost in the shadows – provided they didn't make any sudden movements and provided the moon didn't emerge from behind clouds again.

'You,' Decker said, gesticulating at one of his men, 'check the watch-tower. You, check the storeroom.'

The men disappeared from view while Decker paced round on the spot, more slowly this time, but again his roving gaze passed over Nathan and Jeff then took in the rest of the fort.

Nathan kept still, willing the men to complete their searches quickly, and his hopes were fulfilled when the first man emerged from the tower, shaking his head. He joined Decker in looking around.

A minute passed before the second man returned. Then all three men paced across the roof, looking behind each block and even peering over the edge of the roof to look down into the plaza and then the parade-ground.

Several minutes passed and their actions became more agitated, with Decker throwing his hands high and grumbling before he questioned one of the men again as to what he'd seen. Then they huddled and, with a few murmured comments to each other, they turned to go back down the steps.

Far beyond these men, Nathan had a slim view of the settlement outside the gates and he saw the buildings suddenly glow, that light passing on to the gates and the fort wall.

He looked up to see the first sliver of the moon emerge from behind cloud, the light-level exploding by the moment. He willed Decker to head back down the steps before the moon appeared fully. Beside him Jeff grunted his own low encouragement.

The first man headed down the steps, the second man filing in behind to follow. Decker stayed, looking at the tower, then shrugged and followed them, his form disappearing down into the roof. Nathan watched his body disappear up to his knees with his first step, then two more steps hid him up to the waist until eventually his shoulders and head disappeared from view.

Then the moon emerged, bathing the fort in strong light.

Nathan sighed and turned to Jeff to utter his relief, seeing his friend now in full view, but Jeff was still staring at the tower and his mouth had fallen open. Nathan swung his head to the side to follow the direction of his gaze and saw that Decker had backtracked a step and that his head was now poking out of the wall.

And he was looking directly at them.

'Guards!' he shouted. 'They're over there.'

Even before the moon had slipped back behind the clouds, Nathan and Jeff were on their feet and running. They no longer tried to hide as they put as much distance as they could between themselves and Decker.

The wall led all the way around the fort until it reached the gates. They ran as fast as they could, their only hope to reach the gates, to get to ground level, and then to find somewhere to hide. But even that slim hope disappeared when Decker shouted orders down to the men in the stables and by the time they reached the first corner, a line of men was climbing up a ladder beside the gates.

They skidded to a halt and looked around, searching for another way down to ground level. Nathan couldn't see one. Decker and his guards had now reached the fort wall and the men from the stables had climbed on to the wall beside the gate and were running towards them.

Nathan edged to the side of the wall and peered

down into the parade-ground. The flat roofs of the buildings around the area were below; beyond them there was a substantial drop to the ground. Worse, in response to the commotion Decker had raised, many people had emerged with brands and the parade-ground was well-lit. Many of those people were pointing up at them.

Nathan turned to see that Jeff was peering over the other side of the wall at the land outside the fort.

The drop to the ground was more than thirty feet and Nathan had dismissed that as a viable method of escape. He reckoned that being captured in a few seconds in one piece was preferable to being free for a few minutes but having two broken legs, but Jeff beckoned him to come to the wall.

Nathan joined him and peered over the edge. The ground wasn't visible in the inky darkness below.

'We can't jump,' Nathan said.

'We can. I reckon I can see the ground.' Jeff pointed down into the darkness. 'The wind's pushed dirt up the side of the wall. That'll cushion our fall if we land right next to the wall.'

Nathan peered down, searching for the soft landing that Jeff could see, but saw only the darkness and fluttering after-images of the moon.

'I can't see nothing down there.'

'My hearing is better than yours and my eyesight is better than yours. Trust me.' Jeff stared at the sceptical Nathan then, shrugged. 'Then look at it this way – I've backed all your hunches so far. I reckon it's time you backed one of mine.'

Nathan glanced left and right along the wall. Decker and a trailing line of men were twenty yards away and the group from the gates was slightly further away.

'All right,' he said, climbing on to the short wall. Jeff joined him and they stood swaying before they both looked down. Nathan still couldn't see anything below but darkness. 'But you ought to remember that every hunch I've had so far has led to disaster.'

Jeff winced. 'You just had to remind me of that now.'

They crouched down and rocked back and forth on their heels, building up the courage to leap as the pounding feet of the approaching men closed. Decker shouted out a warning for them to give themselves up.

Jeff glanced at Decker. He shouted out an echoing cry of bravado and defiance, then jumped.

A moment later, Nathan followed him into the darkness.

CHAPTER 5

'Where did they go?'

'Can't see nothing in the dark,' Decker said. 'Bring that brand here.'

Footfalls padded along the top of the wall.

At the base of the wall, Nathan and Jeff pressed their bodies flat to the wall. Jeff's hunch had proved to be correct. Dirt had collected, then arced up the side of the fort, giving them a soft landing in which their legs drove down into the dirt up to their knees.

But they'd had only seconds before Decker peered over the wall and they'd had no time to do anything but stand precisely where they'd landed. As soon as the light Decker had requested arrived, he'd see them, and moving would probably have the same effect.

Nathan glanced at Jeff. In the poor light he saw him shake his head, then press himself against the wall, seeking the best cover he could find. Nathan joined him, seeing the light-level above him grow. Then Decker cried out.

'There they are!'

Nathan winced as he rocked his head to the side to look up, but he couldn't see anyone looking down at them.

'Where?' someone else asked.

'Over there. They're making a run for those rocks. Get out there and head them off.'

Footfalls pounded away along the wall, leaving Nathan and Jeff looking at each other, Jeff's wide open eyes catching a stray beam of light and registering his bemusement.

'I guess,' Nathan whispered, 'Decker got it wrong.'

Jeff nodded, then pointed. Nathan followed his gaze to see movement out on the plains. An unidentifiable night animal was scurrying away.

'Or perhaps our luck is evening out,' Jeff said. 'The moon came out at just the wrong time to let Decker see us, and this time, something moved at just the right time to distract him.'

From further into the fort Nathan heard men shouting as the pursuit started up. So they slipped around the corner of the fort to reach the back and thus be furthest away from the gates. Here, the plains stretched ahead of them, impenetrable in the darkness, but even as they searched for somewhere to hide the light-level was growing and it wasn't from the moon.

People were lighting brands as they emerged from the fort, illuminating the surrounding land. With the fort sitting proudly in the middle of a wide flat area, there was no direction they could go that wouldn't be seen from the tower. And neither of them had any doubt that the tower would now be fully manned with people looking in all directions.

So they moved closer to the wall and lay on their fronts in the loose dirt, then snaked down into it, covering their legs, then bodies, and leaving just their faces peering out.

Nathan didn't hold out much hope that this tactic would work and he reckoned that they were just avoiding the inevitable. But he also reckoned that they had no choice.

In close succession he heard Decker's raised voice coming from the gates, then men galloping off from the fort. Later those men returned, their faint voices sounding low and disgruntled.

Nathan's hopes swelled, but then were dashed when Decker ordered his men to head around the outskirts of the fort and search the surrounding area. With his view limited to just a short stretch of the wall, he could only judge the searchers' positions from the sounds they were making. He heard voices closing, the men walking slowly around the fort. They called to each other as they searched behind any rocks in their path and others frequently hurried off to search further away from the fort.

The procession took ten minutes to walk around the front and side wall before they reached the back wall. Decker's orders and his men's responses confirmed that they were being thorough and Nathan reckoned their capture was imminent.

Even with his limited view, Nathan saw the land beyond the corner lighten up as the brands approached. Every rock stood out in sharp relief as Decker and the first people emerged into his view. They trailed around the corner, but they were walking thirty or so yards from the wall and looking to the plains and not towards their hiding-place at the base of the wall. Then they moved out of Nathan's view as they walked past him and all he could do was listen to them traipse along and hope they wouldn't think to look by the wall.

After they'd passed, they met a noisier group led by the returned Sheriff Buckthorn, which had headed off to circle the fort in the opposite direction.

Around forty yards from where they were hiding they stopped and debated what to do next. Although Nathan couldn't hear everything they said, he heard Decker state that his quarries must have gone back into the fort.

So the search-parties headed off. Nathan heard Jeff murmur a few contented words, but neither man risked talking and instead waited until they were sure they were safe.

The sounds of a search continued unabated for the next hour, then for the next hour intermittently. Then there was silence.

Only then did they emerge from the ground to consider their next actions.

'I just can't believe Decker didn't capture us,' Jeff said, batting the dirt from his clothes.

Nathan shook his head as he considered the arc of light on the western horizon.

'Say that when we've got away from the fort.'

Jeff joined in him considering the light which heralded the start of a new day and which, if they were to stay here, would surely bring capture.

'But how? If we leave now, someone is sure to see us.'

They knocked around their limited options, but with sun-up approaching with every minute, they failed to come up with a plan.

Slipping down under the dirt had worked in the night, but hiding there under the baking heat of the sun without water for the whole day was likely to kill them even if nobody found them. The growing light ensured that just walking away wouldn't work, with the nearest cover being at least a mile away over open land.

And there was nowhere in the fort where they could hide now that they'd drawn attention to who they were and what they'd done.

With still no clear plan in mind, they worked their way around the walls, hoping to come across a different aspect and perhaps see a hiding-place that they could reach. But each corner failed to reveal any cover in any direction and they reached the settlement that surrounded the gates with no ideas coming to them.

Both men were still loath to sneak back into the fort to steal horses, but neither did they have a better idea. So reluctantly, they edged closer to the gates and the settlement.

Sun-up was now imminent and people were stirring. As folk from within the fort had raised most of last night's commotion, they hoped that if any of the people in the settlement saw them they wouldn't view their presence as suspicious.

But they also hoped they wouldn't have to test their luck.

They were within twenty yards of the gates when wheels rattled. Then a wagon emerged through the gates. They were in full view and the driver couldn't help but see them if he looked their way, but he had his gaze set on the trail ahead.

They watched him head away, willing him not to turn round. But although he kept his gaze set forward, he pulled back on the reins, halting the wagon beside the first building on the edge of the settlement.

He called out, a man came out of the building, and the two men chatted with much good-natured gesticulating.

'At least he didn't see us,' Jeff said. 'Let's hope he finishes talking soon and leaves.'

Nathan considered the wagon, noting the heaped bags and stacked crates on the back.

'Or that he carries on talking for long enough for us to get on that wagon.' Nathan grabbed Jeff's arm and tugged, then ran off alongside the wall.

They reached the gates where they were directly behind the wagon and so out of view of both the driver and the man he was talking to. To approach the wagon on a route that would keep them unseen by these men, they'd have to risk being in full view of anyone in the fort who was looking through the gates.

Nathan was stealing himself to glance in and see whether anyone was in the parade-ground when the man returned to his building and, with a short holler from the driver, the wagon trundled off.

Nathan stared at the receding back of the wagon, seeing what was probably their only chance to escape from the fort disappearing and without checking what was behind them, he sprinted off.

Jeff tore along with him and before the wagon built up speed they reached it and rolled over the backboard to land in the wagon. They faced a solid block of crates, but Nathan saw a gap between the two central crates. He crawled through it to emerge on the other side where he pressed himself up against a pile of corn-sacks.

Jeff lay on his side to wriggle in and, with Nathan tugging his shoulders and with him kicking his way on, he squeezed through the gap to join him. The two men shuffled round into the most comfortable positions they could find and considered each other.

'Anyone see us?' Nathan asked, smiling hopefully.

'Didn't look back,' Jeff said, drawing his knees up to his chin, 'but I guess we'll find out soon enough.'

Both men stayed quiet, listening to the wheels trundling round. Nathan reckoned a minute of uninterrupted travel would tell them that the driver hadn't realized they'd stowed away amongst his cargo and that nobody from the fort had seen them climb on board either.

That minute passed slowly and so did the next.

Nathan and Jeff were just looking at each other, smiling and placing their hands to their hearts in mock relief, when a voice cut through the rattling of the wheels.

'Stop right there!' the stentorian voice intoned.

'Now,' another voice said from ahead, presumably the driver's, 'since when have you had the right to order me around?'

An arrogant snort sounded. 'Mayor Decker's orders.'

The wheels slowed to a halt as Nathan and Jeff lowered their heads, wincing as they awaited their inevitable capture.

'Orders or no orders, I still got a delivery to make in Hope Creek today and Providence tomorrow, and no matter what you say, I plan to make them both.'

An irritated grunt sounded and through the thin sliver that was available to Nathan's view, he saw a horse trot past.

'And you still can.' The voice now sounded as if the rider was standing alongside the driver. 'I just need to ask you a few questions.'

In the wagon, Nathan raised his head and looked at Jeff, who also raised his head and mouthed that they hadn't been seen, after all. This man was just checking up on everybody who left the fort.

Nathan nodded then shuffled down to press himself into the sacks, as did Jeff, as they maximized their chances that a quick search would fail to reveal them.

'Then hurry up and ask those questions.'

'Two outlaws broke Kenton Taylor out of jail last night, but they didn't get away. You seen them?'

The driver snorted a laugh. 'So it's true. They broke him out of jail, but couldn't get themselves out of the fort. What kind of idiots are they?'

'The kind that are still at large and they're formidable. They fought their way into the jailhouse, defeated Sheriff Buckthorn in a fierce gun battle, and broke Kenton out.'

'And you said all that with a straight face. What really happened? Did Buckthorn drink himself into a stupor again and Kenton just walked out?'

'The official story is that two desperadoes broke him out after a fierce gun battle, and don't forget it.'

There was a short pause, then the driver laughed, the other man joining him.

'I won't. But don't you worry about me. I got me a gun and if I meet the men who were formidable enough to defeat Sheriff Buckthorn, I reckon as I can defend myself.'

'You do that,' the man said with laughter in his tone. He lowered his voice. 'But just remember – they're still outlaws, called Nathan Palmer and Jeff Morgan. Tell everyone you meet that Mayor Decker is offering two hundred dollars a head on them.'

Then he swung his horse past the wagon and hoofs clopped as he headed back to the fort. The wagon lurched to a start and headed off again.

After having had several false hopes of escape dashed, Nathan steeled himself for the man to return or for someone else to chase after them, but ten minutes passed without them being called back. Only then did he relax and risk smiling at Jeff again.

'Looks like we've made it,' Nathan said, with a mock wipe of the sweat from his brow.

'Yeah,' Jeff said. He edged to the side to look through the gap, back towards the fort. 'And we learnt something from that exchange.'

'I know,' Nathan murmured, joining Jeff in peering through the gap between the crates. They were now at least a mile from the fort. 'We're wanted men.'

Jeff flinched back to consider him.

'Nathan, I've heard that tone before and that had better be the last time. We can't go back to the fort to get that money, or to free that prisoner, or to do whatever other plans are going on in that curious mind of yours. You know that.'

Nathan continued to look at the fort, imagining what it would be like to be the man imprisoned in the tower, then shook himself and looked away.

'Yeah,' he said, 'we can't go back to the fort.'

Muscle-rending cramps had set in some time since Nathan heard the driver speak for the first time in a while. He didn't hear his words as the driver called out to someone, and shortly afterwards a rider passed going in the opposite direction. Presently another rider passed, the sudden bustle around them suggesting they were closing on Hope Creek.

They had been travelling for most of the day, with

the driver making only brief stops. They hadn't dared to use those stops to move positions and although sacks and crates of edibles surrounded them, their raging thirsts were controlling their thoughts. But both men had agreed they wouldn't come out until they reached somewhere where they could seek proper shelter.

As they passed a building and then another, they shuffled closer to each other.

'Is Hope Creek far enough away from the fort?' Jeff asked.

Nathan clapped his parched mouth then rubbed his calves again.

'Only thing on my mind is whether thirst or cramps are going to kill me first. So I reckon we got no choice but to hope it is.'

'And then what?' Jeff raised his eyebrows.

'If you're asking me whether I want to go back to Fort Benton, then I'll say I don't reckon we can. We just have to forget we ever got that key or heard about that money or saw that man in the tower.' Nathan watched Jeff sigh with relief then leaned forward. 'But not just yet.'

Jeff winced. 'Why not?'

'Because we're wanted men. And that means we got to put right what we did wrong by finding Kenton Taylor and taking him back to the law.'

Jeff's eyebrows shot up. 'In Fort Benton?'

'No, just to the nearest law, but we can't go back to our old way of life with a wanted notice following us around.'

Jeff lowered his head, sighing, then looked up and shook his head.

'I guess that won't be healthy, but we ain't got much

chance of finding him with no money, no guns, no horses and with everyone after us.' Jeff sat up straight. 'So unless you got an idea as to how we catch him while we got all those problems, we have to put him out of our minds and find ourselves some honest work instead.'

Nathan considered Jeff's firm jaw and despite his reluctance to agree, he had to admit he'd taken most of the recent decisions and they'd all been bad ones. He nodded and with that agreement, they shuffled through the gap in the crates to the back of the wagon. They had reached Hope Creek's main road. As nobody was out on the length of road that they could see, they rolled out of the wagon and ran to a halt. Then they stood crouched, slowly righting themselves and freeing the creaks from their bones.

They straightened as the wagon drew away, but half-way down the road it stopped outside a store. So they shuffled away to lean back against the nearest wall and chatted animatedly about their predicament, neither man looking at the wagon as they tried to create the impression they had been in town for some time.

They hadn't been talking for long when the only movement out on the road drew their gazes. Outside the livery stables a rider was dismounting. Then he went into the stables, pausing just long enough to let his horse dunk its head in a trough beside the doors.

They headed across the road and, without embarrassment, dunked their heads in the rank water, oblivious to the scum as they enjoyed the coolness. Only when the bitter taste was making them gag did they tear themselves away. While Jeff rescued his hat from the trough and slopped it back on his head, Nathan looked into the stables.

Plenty of horses were lined up in the stalls and far more than he'd expect in such a small town. The man who had just entered was leading his horse into a stall at the far end and either the stable-owner was elsewhere or this man was the owner, because nobody emerged to help him.

As the man located a bag of corn, Nathan pointed him out to Jeff, who without preamble headed inside.

'You know who owns this fine establishment?' he called out.

'I do,' the man said, without turning, then introduced himself as Quincy Lackey, the owner.

Jeff looked at Nathan, who beckoned for him to continue taking the lead. So Jeff embarked on his speech about looking for work, this time with sincerity, but Quincy soon turned and shook his head.

'Are you sure?' Jeff persisted. 'You got plenty of horses to look after here.'

Quincy still shook his head and Jeff looked at Nathan, his raised eyebrows asking whether he should persist, but Nathan ignored him. Half-way down the row of stalls one horse had caught his attention – his own. It even had his saddle-bag dangling over the back of the stall.

'You may not want our help,' he said, setting his feet wide, 'but we're mighty interested to know where you get your horses.'

Quincy broke off from tending to his horse to pace across the stables. He stood before them and considered their threadbare and bedraggled state.

'You can't compete with me.'

'We can't. We just want to know where you got one

particular horse.' Nathan pointed his horse out and Jeff followed his gaze, gulped, then slammed his wide hands on his hips and joined Nathan in glaring at Quincy.

Quincy flicked the merest of glances at the horse, then considered both men's belligerent stances without any sign of concern crossing his blank expression.

'My sources are my concern.'

'Horse-thieving is a mighty serious offence.' Nathan edged a pace to the side as if he were about to leave. 'Perhaps we ought to find a lawman and see what he has to say.'

'Perhaps you should, because earlier today I heard that two desperadoes had broken an outlaw out of Fort Benton's jail. I can ask that lawman if he reckons those men are you.'

Nathan firmed his jaw. 'You can, because from what I've heard, those men are only looking at a stretch in jail, but a horse-thief is looking at a stretched neck.' Nathan paced up to Quincy and met his gaze. 'So I ask you again – where did you get that horse?'

For long moments the two men stared at each. With the icy conviction brought on by the traumatic events of the last day behind Nathan's gaze, and with Jeff looming at his shoulder, Quincy was the first to look away.

'Just that one?' he asked.

'Just that one.'

Quincy looked at Nathan's horse, rubbing his jaw, then shrugged.

'I bought that steed in good faith.'

'Then perhaps you'd like to sell it back to me in good faith.'

Quincy nodded. 'How much you offering?'

Nathan tipped out his pockets. 'Nothing. You see the man you bought it off stole everything we had.'

'Then I can't help you.' Quincy turned away.

'But,' Jeff said, striding forward to stand before Nathan, 'we must be able to reach an agreement.'

Quincy turned back then let his gaze rise to consider Jeff, who lifted his heels to peer down at Quincy from an even greater height. He even flexed his arms and fists for added encouragement.

Quincy flinched then backed away a pace to look down the stables, a foot tapping on the ground. He murmured something to himself then swung back to consider them.

'Perhaps,' he said, 'there is one way.'

They had been riding since first light and it'd require the rest of the day before they'd reach Shinbone. Quincy rode up front while Nathan and Jeff rode behind him.

Yesterday, Quincy had acted reasonably in giving them a place to sleep and a meal and his offer to return Nathan's horse if they helped him deliver fifteen horses to Shinbone had been a fair one they couldn't decline.

Nathan glanced back at the line of five horses he was leading and sighed, then looked at Jeff, who was grinning.

'What you looking so pleased about?' Nathan asked.

Jeff glanced ahead to confirm Quincy was too far ahead to hear him.

'We're doing honest work again, and that sure feels good.'

'I guess,' Nathan said, then looked ahead.

They had left Texas to search for honest work and

the thought of the $10,000 in Fort Benton had distracted them awhile, but Jeff was right. Now that they stood no chance of getting that money, they were free to return their thoughts to their previous aims.

But no matter how much Nathan tried to convince himself that he had to forget the money and the prisoner in the tower, his thoughts kept returning to Fort Benton.

Admittedly, neither the money nor the prisoner's plight was their concern, but only they knew about him and so only they could free him. So later, when they drew up to water the horses and take a break, Nathan dragged Quincy into conversation.

Before long, he steered him round to talking about Fort Benton.

'You deal much with the fort?' he asked.

'Mainly with Shinbone and Providence,' Quincy said, 'and further east.'

'Fort not a profitable place, then?'

Jeff flashed Nathan the kind of wide-eyed glare Nathan gave to Jeff when he was being unsubtle, but Nathan ignored him.

Quincy considered his answer before turning to Nathan.

'You're mighty interested about Fort Benton.'

'Curious, you could say.'

Jeff snorted to himself as Quincy looked off down the trail towards Shinbone, then back towards Hope Creek and Fort Benton.

'Now, I hired you boys because I took you on your word that you weren't outlaws, but if there's anything you want to say, I'll tell you this: if you aim to bush-whack me, neither of you has a gun, and I can take care of myself.' He flashed a smile. 'And if that wasn't your intent, then remember I did buy your horse off Kenton Taylor, knowing he was running from the law, so I won't turn you in.'

Nathan nodded, avoiding displaying any emotion.

'That's mighty generous of you if you were to come across those men. There's a two hundred dollar bounty on each man.'

Quincy leaned towards Nathan and winked.

'There is, but I don't like who I'd have to collect it off, and I don't reckon many people would believe they'll see that money if they were to find those ruthless outlaws.' Quincy looked them up and down, a smile twitching his lips.

Nathan sighed. 'Well, I can tell you one thing for sure – we ain't no ruthless outlaws!'

'You ain't or I wouldn't have hired you, but you did come from Fort Benton and you were hungry and desperate. And Kenton Taylor looked even more desperate. I guess I owed you something after dealing with him.'

'You did.'

'I'll take that for an admittance you are those men.' Quincy tipped back his hat. 'What happened? Did Kenton break out of jail on his own while Sheriff Buckthorn was in a drunken stupor and you two just happened to be the nearest to the jailhouse.'

'I guess that pretty much sums it up.' Nathan shrugged. 'And from what I saw, Mayor Decker was the man in control there. I can't see why he accepts having such an incompetent sheriff.'

'He needs a fool like him around so that he can run things the way he wants. And the way he's buying up every scrap of land, all for the lowest price a bit of healthy intimidation can get him, it won't be long before he's running his own empire there in Fort Benton.'

'If he's that ruthless, does that mean Kenton Taylor might not be the man who killed Frank Reed?'

'I've got no idea, but that's what I'll tell my conscience.'

Nathan considered before he asked his next question, and although Jeff was shooting harsh glares at him, he asked it anyhow.

'How would anyone take on Decker?'

As Quincy considered his answer, Jeff jumped to his feet and stomped to his side to loom over him, but Nathan avoided meeting his eye.

'My advice would be to just stay away from him.' Quincy paused when Jeff grunted his agreement, before continuing. 'You boys are wanted men, but nobody but Decker will pursue you for it. I reckon you should just think yourself lucky you escaped from Fort Benton and keep on heading away. And now, we got some horses to get to Shinbone by sundown.'

Quincy stood and paced away, leaving Jeff looking at Nathan.

'Like the man said,' Jeff said, walking round to stand before Nathan. 'We should think ourselves lucky and concentrate on getting these horses to Shinbone, right?'

'Yeah,' Nathan said not meeting Jeff's eye.

'You didn't sound like you really meant that,' Jeff persisted.

Nathan removed the key from his pocket and turned it over then looked up at Jeff. While meeting his eyes, he opened his hand and let the key fall to the ground.

'I do,' he said. 'I've had enough of Fort Benton, too. I just had to know about the situation back there before I could move on.'

Jeff slapped Nathan's arm then headed to the horses.

Nathan watched him leave and when he was sure he wouldn't look back, he swooped down and scooped up the key.

Night was drawing in by the time they rode into Shinbone.

Nathan had done plenty of thinking and although he'd kept the key, with every mile they put between themselves and Fort Benton, the urge to return lessened and the events of the last few days felt less important.

What Jeff had said and what Quincy had advised was right. They were lucky to have escaped and even if Decker was building his own empire in Fort Benton, it really did have nothing to do with them.

So when they'd taken the horses to their destination on the outskirts of Shinbone, and Quincy told them to stay outside the stables while he completed his dealings, Nathan fingered the key in his pocket with some embarrassment. He vowed that when his friend happened to be looking elsewhere, he would really dispose of it, and he had no problem in answering honestly when Jeff asked what was worrying him.

'I guess I've finally accepted you're right,' he said. 'Once we have my horse back, we'll get on it, ride on out of here and keep going until we find work. And we won't look back.'

Jeff raised his hands high then slapped them down on his thighs.

'And I sure am pleased to hear that, at last.' He patted Nathan's back. 'Honest work and no worrying about other people's gunfights, and money hidden in forts, and prisoners in cells, and prisoners in towers is just about right for us.'

Nathan nodded and together they waited for Quincy to come out. Presently, Quincy left the stables, tucking a wad of bills into his pocket and beaming.

'Struck a good deal?' Nathan asked.

'Sure did,' Quincy said, patting his pocket. 'And that horse is now yours – again.'

'Obliged.'

'And you two worked hard today.' Quincy reached into his pocket, then counted out four dollar bills and slapped them into Nathan's hand. 'Take that as well and buy yourself a meal and a drink.'

'Even more obliged, and if you're so satisfied, could you use the services of two hard-working men?'

'Nope.' Quincy rubbed his jaw as he considered them, then pointed out of town. 'But as the nearest town is Providence, about fifty miles south of here, I assume you'll be heading further east.'

'Sure will. We're not risking meeting Kenton Taylor again.'

'Then you're being sensible. You'll get to Dodge City in two days, maybe three. You could try Carter Jones there. He's a bigger horse-trader than I am. I can't say whether he'll have work available or whether he'll want to hire you, but just mention my name and that you did good work for me. It'll give you a place to start.'

Nathan and Jeff tipped their hats and thanked him. While Quincy rode off, they turned to look down the road. They debated whether to stay in town and get that meal and drink, or whether to buy provisions from the store and cook for themselves.

Despite the mouth-watering aroma of sizzling steak coming from somewhere and the lively chatter emerging from the saloon, they agreed that staying out of people's sight when they were still so close to Fort Benton was the best plan.

So they looked around for the store, but whereas Jeff continued turning until he located it, Nathan's gaze stopped at the saloon.

'Come on,' Jeff said. 'We agreed to move on and not go to the saloon.'

'We did, but we can't move on just yet.'

Nathan pointed, drawing Jeff's attention to the line of horses at the hitching-rail. The horse furthest from them was Jeff's horse.

'Kenton Taylor is in the saloon,' Jeff said, his eyes flaring.

'Yeah,' Nathan said then set off down the road, 'and even if we are moving on, we've got unfinished business with him.'

CHAPTER 6

Nathan walked at a determined pace towards the saloon with Jeff hurrying to catch up with him. He reached the boardwalk and stomped to a halt in the doorway.

With his hands holding on to the batwings, he roved his gaze around the room. A dozen or so men were within, most playing or watching a poker-game by the side wall, but Nathan's gaze quickly alighted on the man sitting alone at the back nursing a coffee.

This man had his hat pulled down low and didn't look at them as most of the other people did, but even with his limited view of his features, Nathan was sure it was Kenton.

He glanced over his shoulder. He received a nod. With Jeff a pace behind him, he headed across the room and swung to a halt before the table looking down at Kenton. Although Nathan's shadow fell across the table, Kenton didn't look up, but Nathan saw his hand tense then shift to the edge of table. Nathan noted he was wearing the initialled gun.

Nathan waited. Slowly Kenton raised his head to look at him. Long before his gaze reached Nathan's face, he nodded with recognition.

'Howdy, Nathan,' he said. 'It seems you found me.'

'We sure did.'

'You did well.' He flashed a grin, then let a deep scowl contort his features before he lowered his head again. 'Now, leave me.'

'You know we can't do that. We broke you out of jail and yet you stole everything we had and left us to face a whole heap of trouble back in Fort Benton.'

'I did you a favour. The likes of you would never have seen off a posse. I gave you a chance to get away while I lost them.'

Nathan snorted. 'That's a lie and you know it.'

'Perhaps.' Kenton laughed then looked up, showing no sign of humour in his cold eyes. 'But think of this – I did you a favour by not killing you. Now, unless you want to call me out into the road and get yourself all filled with holes, leave.'

Nathan gestured back at Jeff. 'There's two of us.'

Kenton's gaze flicked up to Jeff then cupped a hand around his mug.

'You still got only the one gun between you.'

'But we aren't going nowhere until you answer our questions.' Nathan waited for a response, but Kenton just sipped his coffee. 'We want to know who really killed Frank Reed. We want to know why you were to face a firing-squad on Wednesday. We want to know about—'

'Nathan,' Jeff urged from behind him, 'we only came for our horse.'

Nathan shook his head, now feeling the pent-up irritations of the last few days welling up inside.

'Just talk,' he grunted.

Kenton took another sip before he replied.

'Answers to questions like those ain't got nothing to

do with you.'

'But they have got plenty to do with you.' Nathan softened his voice. 'And no matter how often you threaten us, I reckon you're not the outlaw you appeared to be back in Fort Benton.'

Kenton laughed. This time his amusement reached his eyes before he blinked it away.

'Don't risk finding out.'

'I will, because you're just being too tolerant for a man who they say killed Frank Reed. So answer my questions and then tell me about the subject Jeff didn't want me to mention – the ten thousand dollars.'

Kenton tensed, his sudden hand-twitch making the mug slip from his hand and splash coffee over the table.

'Go away.'

Nathan leaned down to the table, placing his hands flat to the wood and sharing Kenton's eye-line.

'I ain't and while you're talking, you can tell me about Decker's prisoner in the tower.'

Kenton narrowed his eyes as he looked straight into Nathan's eyes.

'What's it to you?'

'Nothing. We just want to know what's happening back at Fort Benton.'

For long moments they glared at each with their faces just inches apart. Nathan heard Jeff shuffling from foot to foot as he resisted the urge to drag him away and leave. He could also sense the eyes of everyone in the saloon on them and he reckoned that scrutiny more than anything else would prey on Kenton's mind. Sure enough, Kenton flinched back.

'Not here,' he said and stood. Without further word he walked past them and headed to the door.

'What you go and raise all that for?' Jeff said when Kenton had left the saloon. 'I thought we were getting my horse off him, then moving on.'

'We were, but like you keep telling me, I'm just plain too curious for my own good.'

Four miles out of Shinbone, Kenton headed off the trail. He rode alongside a series of increasingly large boulders until he reached a grouping of two huge boulders, a line of small rocks set before them providing a semicircular shelter.

As agreed, Nathan and Jeff followed 200 yards back as they ensured nobody followed them out of town.

When they joined Kenton he was sitting on one of the rocks and looking at the plains, the gathering darkness isolating him. He gestured for them to sit with him. Nathan saw that in the gap between the huge boulders and the smaller rocks there were several circles of blackened stones, suggesting this was a common place for travellers to make camp.

'All right,' Kenton said, leaning on his knees to consider them, 'give me a straight answer or I'll tell you nothing. Why do you want to know?'

Jeff shrugged then gestured for Nathan to answer. Nathan picked up a handful of dirt and sprinkled it through his fingers while he put his thoughts in order.

'I guess,' he said, 'the answer is it really has nothing to do with us, but we heard a rumour about ten thousand dollars being in the fort. We got it into our heads that freeing you would get us that money as a reward. It didn't.'

'And do you still want that money?'

Nathan glanced at the scowling Jeff before replying.

'Nope. We're wanted men in Fort Benton so we're moving on.'

'So why do you care about any of this?'

Jeff spoke up. 'Because you stole my horse and we ain't leaving here until you—'

'Yeah, yeah, I know, but I don't reckon that's Nathan's main concern.'

Nathan considered. Caring about the plight of a prisoner he'd only seen for a few seconds wasn't a good answer, and as he didn't want to annoy Jeff any more than he already had, he settled for a compromise.

'We broke you out of jail and if someone ever comes looking for us, we'd like to know whether you're a guilty man or an innocent man.'

'Then I'll tell you this,' Kenton said. 'I'm guilty of plenty, but I didn't kill Frank Reed.'

'Can you prove it?'

Kenton provided a wry smile. 'I could, but not just yet.'

'Then who did kill him?'

Kenton stood and paraded around on the spot, his firm jaw suggesting he was debating whether to answer.

'Nobody killed him,' he said at last. 'He's still alive. That's why it'll be easy after Wednesday to prove I didn't do it.' Kenton snorted a harsh chuckle. 'Frank's the prisoner in the tower.'

Nathan looked aloft, nodding. 'Some of this is starting to fit together, but what I don't understand is, if that's true, why did you leave him there?'

'Until you mentioned him in the saloon, I didn't know where Decker was hiding him, but once I've gathered together the rest of my folk, I will go back for him.'

'And you'll do that by Wednesday?'

'You got it.'

'And why then?'

'You got an awful lot of questions in you for a man who's just moving on and doesn't care about this. Will it stop those questions if I say you'll never get your hands on the ten thousand dollars?'

'But it does exist?'

'Nope, that was Decker's offer to Frank and me for our land. We turned it down and that's why he took Frank prisoner and tried to destroy me by claiming I killed him.' Kenton turned to stare into the descending darkness, not offering any more details. After waiting a polite amount of time Jeff spoke up to offer more encouragement.

'We know your family and the Reeds feuded for years,' he said, 'and that that ended when Frank married your sister. Is Decker trying to take advantage of that situation?'

Kenton didn't reply immediately. When he did eventually speak his voice was low and resigned and had none of the arrogance he'd shown earlier.

'It's common knowledge we ended our feud, but what ain't commonly known is the deal our fathers did to ensure it really would end for good. They wrote in their wills that a year and a day after the last of them died, Frank and me would have to draw up a new title to our land to combine our ranches into one. If we didn't, we'd have to put all the land up to auction.'

'And did you draw up that title?'

'We did, but we didn't figure on Decker stopping us registering it. His office is the land office and we have to report there by three o'clock on Wednesday, a year and a day after Frank's father died, or the land goes to the highest bidder. You can guess the rest. With me in jail and with Frank in the tower, we couldn't stop the land going to auction, and Decker will ensure he's the only bidder. It'll fetch one hell of a lot less than ten thousand dollars.'

'But now that you're free, you'll register?'

'Sure will, but I'll get Frank out first. I don't want Decker taking out his rage on him.' Kenton turned to them. 'Anything you can tell me about what you saw in that tower will be appreciated.'

Nathan nodded and reached into his pocket for the key.

'Hey,' Jeff shouted. 'You threw that . . . Oh, you'll just never learn, will you?'

'Nope.' Nathan patted Jeff's shoulder until he returned a smile, then held out the key. 'Take it.'

Kenton took the key. It might have been a sudden cooling breeze passing over him, but that simple action relaxed the tension from Nathan's shoulders. Then Nathan described the layout of the tower and the space he'd seen behind the wall.

Kenton nodded frequently and rechecked the details. Then he turned away and rocked his head from side to side.

'You got a plan in mind?' Nathan asked.

'Not yet. I'm guessing Decker locked Frank in there so that he can hear him taking control of our land. It ain't enough for that man to win. He has to see his victims suffer. But if I can get in and get him out . . .'

Kenton continued to look down the trail towards Shinbone, but then he swirled round to glare at Nathan, his eyes opening wide.

'I'll tell you anything you want to know,' Nathan said.

'And you can keep the horse now that we—'

'I don't care about that,' Kenton roared, his gaze darting up to look over Nathan's shoulder. 'You brought Decker with you.'

Nathan swirled round and saw that 300 yards down the trail, seven riders were thundering towards them. They were still too far away to see who they were, but Nathan was sure Kenton was right and the lead man was Decker.

'We didn't lead Decker to you,' Nathan said, backing away from Kenton.

'I don't believe that,' Kenton snapped. 'I know I abandoned you in Fort Benton, but I was desperate. I didn't think you'd repay me like this.'

'We're not repaying you for what you did, because we're fighting with you against him.'

Kenton continued to glare at them, but as a gunshot from the advancing men whistled into the rocks to his side, he vaulted over the rocks and hunkered down on the other side.

Jeff and Nathan jumped over to join him and although both men looked at Kenton, hoping to discuss tactics, he didn't look at either man. Instead, he crawled away in the opposite direction, seeking the more substantial cover of the larger rocks to the side.

Nathan raised himself to peer over the rocks and saw that Decker and his men were gaining cover behind a tangle of rocks about forty yards away. Those rocks joined onto the line of boulders that arced round until they reached the two huge boulders between which they were hiding. Nathan reckoned it wouldn't be long before Decker ordered his men to take positions on top of those boulders and surround them.

'Time to give yourself up, Kenton,' Decker shouted

from behind his cover, the delight in his tone evident.

'Go to hell,' Kenton shouted.

'You'll go there first unless you come out now.'

'I'd sooner die here than face your firing-squad back in Fort Benton.'

Decker laughed aloud. 'That's pretty much what Frank Reed said, just before I killed him.'

Kenton shot a glance at Nathan, urging him with flared eyes to be quiet and not reveal that he knew Frank was still alive. Nathan returned a downwards calming gesture with his hands, conveying that he realized that Decker was trying to goad him into acting rashly.

'Frank always was impetuous,' Kenton said, his tone calm. 'He probably had it coming to him. Me, I just want to return to Providence.'

'I can't let you do that – unless you accept my deal – five thousand dollars.'

'It was ten thousand last week.'

'And it'll keep going down until that deadline passes. Then, it'll go to the highest bidder and that'll be me.' Decker raised himself as he laughed, the sound echoing amongst the rocks. 'I reckon one dollar should see off all opposition.'

'You won't get away with this!' Kenton bobbed up and fired at Decker, his wild gunfire forcing him to dive for cover.

'I'll take that for your answer,' Decker shouted, hidden from view. 'And before you threaten me again remember my quarrel is just with you, Kenton. If your friends want to leave, I'll let them go.'

Kenton snorted, then quickly crawled along the ground to join Nathan.

'Ignore that. He won't let any of us get out of this alive.'

'We know,' Nathan said, 'and know this – we're with you.'

Kenton reached into his pocket for the gun he'd taken off Jeff two days ago.

'Then we got to . . .' Kenton looked over Nathan's shoulder. 'Where's your friend?'

Nathan looked around and saw that Kenton was right. While Kenton and Decker were trading taunts, Jeff had slipped away into the gloom.

'Don't worry,' he said. 'Jeff's slow to get involved in fights but when he does, he sure ends them quickly. I'm guessing he's sneaked off to earn us a distraction.'

Kenton bobbed up to look around, peering into the gloom.

'Decker will make his move soon, so while Jeff's doing that, we have to find a way out of here. We'll start by getting closer to Decker.' Kenton pointed. 'You cover me while I head over there. Then I'll cover you.'

Nathan looked ahead, seeing several boulders lying between them and Decker's position, but not welcoming the thought of the dash over twenty yards of bare ground to reach them. He was about to shake his head when a cry sounded from the huge boulder to their side.

Then a man tumbled backwards over the top of the boulder, rolling before he hit the ground. A second man followed, flying sideways with his head rocked backwards. Jeff appeared briefly with a fist raised, having slugged the man's jaw before he dropped out of view.

'At least we know where Jeff is now,' Nathan said.

Kenton grunted his approval. 'And he's reduced the number of men we're facing. That just leaves Decker and four other men now. I prefer those odds. Now, come on. I'm taking Decker out before he makes a move on me.'

Kenton didn't wait for a reply. He jumped to his feet, vaulted over the boulder and hurried off towards the nearest covering rock. Nathan did as requested and covered him with a burst of gunfire, keeping Decker down. Kenton kept his head down and ran as fast he could before skidding to a halt behind the rock.

The moment Kenton came to a halt, he started firing at Decker's position, pinning Decker and his men down. Nathan leapt over his covering line of rocks and hurried on to reach the next scrap of safe cover, a sprawling line of boulders about fifteen yards to Kenton's side and twenty yards from Decker.

He skidded into position behind them, then lay down, reloading. To his side, Kenton did the same, then raised his hand with the fingers wide, flexing the hand three times to show he'd run for the next cover in fifteen seconds.

Nathan took that time to look for Jeff, searching for him in his prowl through the gloom and hoping he had more of Decker's men in his sights. He considered each of the boulders to his side before his wandering gaze picked him out, kneeling beside a boulder. He raised a hand to acknowledge him, but then saw that Jeff was looking down with his hands held high.

Nathan winced, just as cold metal jabbed into his back. A voice whispered in his ear.

'Any sudden moves and you die.'

Nathan glanced back to see a man lying behind him, his arm outstretched to thrust the gun into his back. Nathan gave a slight nod, then remembered Kenton and flinched round, but his assailant was lying out of Kenton's view and so he wouldn't be able to see his predicament. With mounting horror, Nathan saw Kenton counting down the last few seconds before he'd run.

Then he was on his feet and running for the next cover, five yards before Decker's position. He'd run for five paces before he darted a glance towards Nathan, his firm jaw demanding to know why he wasn't covering him, but Nathan could do nothing but watch him run and hope he'd get lucky.

As it was, Kenton had barely halved the distance from his intended destination when two men jumped up to confront him with guns drawn. On the run, Kenton swung his gun round to aim at the nearest, but before he could fire, a burst of gunfire ripped out from both men, scything into Kenton's chest and cutting him off. At least four shots hammered into him before Kenton keeled over into the dirt to lie face down. He didn't return a single shot.

Nathan lowered his head. A grunt and an encouraging jab in the back forced him to throw his gun down, then stand. To his side, the man holding Jeff forced him to stand too.

Decker stood from his hiding-place. He sported a wide grin as he beckoned for the men holding Nathan and Jeff to drag them out into the open. Neither captive met the other man's eye as they stomped to a halt a few paces from Kenton's body.

Decker knelt to check on Kenton, his twinkling eyes betraying only delight as he kicked him over to lie sprawled on his back. Even so, he couldn't restrain himself from swinging a firm kick into the dead man's ribs before he turned to face Jeff and Nathan.

'Go on,' Nathan said, raising his chin and glaring at him. 'Shoot us and be done with it.'

'Can't see that the likes of you are worth the risk,' Decker said, sneering at them. 'Kenton was an escaped outlaw and everyone will reckon he deserved what he got, but you're just two bodies too many to explain.'

'They helped Kenton escape,' one of his men said.

'They did, but nobody will believe they're the desperadoes Buckthorn claimed broke into the jail. Look at them.' Decker gestured round at his men, encouraging them to gloat at his prisoners' predicament. 'Do they look dangerous?'

'Only to themselves,' one man said.

Decker chuckled. 'Just let them go. I've had all the use I'll get out of them.' Decker paced up to Nathan and looked him up and down. 'You didn't really reckon you'd escaped from Fort Benton, did you?'

Nathan winced. 'You mean you followed us?'

'Sure did. After you leapt off the wall, you were stupid enough to just stand still, hoping I couldn't see you. Then you hid in the dirt for most of the night. Then you hid in a wagon. Then you . . . Do I need to go on?'

'I guess not.'

'You two were too worthless to bother catching, but I had a hunch that bumbling fools like you would lead me to Kenton. I doubt you actually found him as such. You probably just stumbled across him, but I don't care, letting you think you'd escaped paid off in the end.' Decker slapped a hand on both men's shoulders. 'Now, as a reward for delivering Kenton to me, you have my permission to get out of my sight.'

'You're really letting us go?' Nathan heard himself ask, then immediately regretted giving Decker the satisfaction of hearing his relief.

'Sure am.' Decker shoved both men forward then pointed off down the trail in the opposite direction to Fort Benton. 'But just make sure you ride off that-a-way and keep on riding. If I ever see you again, you will face that firing-squad.'

Decker stared at Nathan, then Jeff. Then he turned and without looking back headed to his horse. His men stayed back to gather the two men Jeff had knocked out and shake them awake. These men also muttered their contempt for Nathan and Jeff and what they'd do to them if they ever saw them again.

Then they rode off, leaving them alone with Kenton's dead body.

'He didn't reckon we were worth killing,' Jeff murmured, watching Decker's back recede into the gloom.

'Can't complain about that, I suppose.' Nathan ground his fists then whipped off his hat and slapped it to the ground. 'But that's the biggest mistake he'll ever make.'

Jeff turned to him. 'You're not thinking of going after him, are you?'

'I sure am and I going to wipe that . . .' Nathan closed his eyes and took deep breaths. A more realistic attitude gradually conquered his anger. 'Nope. I guess not.'

'Then what are we going to do?'

Nathan looked at Kenton's body. 'Kenton's death is our fault. We can't make amends with him now, but there's one thing we can do before we leave.'

*

The sun had risen on a clear Monday morning when Nathan and Jeff rode into Providence. They asked around for directions and after receiving a few sombre glances at the body over the back of Jeff's horse, they were directed to the Bar T ranch.

Nobody approached them as they rode across the ranch land, but when they'd splashed through a river and ridden through a grove of oak, they acquired a cortège of ranch hands. By the time they faced the gates before the ranch house, a dozen men rode around them. None of them as much as asked what had happened, their downcast eyes seeming to accept that Kenton's dead body would return one day.

When they drew up before the house and dismounted, one hand hurried off into the house and emerged with a woman. Nathan assumed she was Nancy, Kenton's sister, and everyone removed their hats as she paced towards the horse, her pained eyes taking in the body lying over the horse. She bent to look up at his face. She closed her eyes and murmured something under her breath, then stood straight to face them.

'Where did you find him?' she asked.

They'd debated what they should say and they'd decided to relate the full truth. So covering the details in a matter-of-fact manner, Nathan told her of how they'd help Kenton escape and how they'd inadvertently led Decker to him afterwards.

Like her brother, she was slow to respond when he'd completed their story.

'That wasn't your fault,' she said at last. 'I'm grateful to you for having brought him back.'

106

'We do have some good news, though.' Nathan forced a smile, hoping to lift Nancy's spirits, but received only a blank expression. 'Your husband is still alive.'

Nancy closed her eyes, placing a hand to heart.

'Then I am blessed. Have you seen him?'

'Yeah. He's in Fort Benton. I only saw him for a moment but he . . .' Nathan searched for a comforting word. 'He looked like he was surviving.'

'I thank you for that information.'

'But you don't have much time. After Wednesday, Decker won't have no need to keep him prisoner any more. He'll probably have to dispose of—'

Nancy raised a hand, silencing him. 'I said I was grateful you brought my brother back to me, but you will leave us now.'

'But Kenton told us plenty before he died and about how you have to register your land title by three o'clock on Wednesday and how—'

'Leave us,' she snapped, her eyes blazing, although whether her anger was directed at them, Decker, or perhaps even her brother, Nathan couldn't tell.

With that she turned her back and, with two of the ranch hands carrying her brother's body behind her, headed into the ranch house. Nathan and Jeff watched her leave until only one man remained. He was the oldest person they'd seen and Nathan reckoned he was the ramrodder.

'I assume you'll try to free Frank,' Nathan said. 'We have plenty of information that'll help.'

'Ain't your place to assume anything,' the man said, his tone low. 'Just do what Nancy said and leave us.'

'Then perhaps you don't understand what you have to do. You can't just ignore what'll happen on

Wednesday. If you don't register, Decker will have the legal right to—'

'And you didn't listen to what she said. Go now or I'll run you off our land.'

Then he turned and headed off into the ranch, leaving Jeff and Nathan alone. They stood in shock for a full minute before Jeff spoke.

'I guess we'd better go,' he said, slapping his hat back on his head.

Nathan hadn't known what kind of reception they'd receive when they returned Kenton's body, but he hadn't expected them to be ignored then told to leave. He sighed and, with Jeff, mounted up his horse and rode slowly away from the Bar T. Occasionally he looked back, but nobody emerged to check they were leaving.

They rode for around thirty minutes, by which time they'd reached the river and the ranch was out of sight. There they stopped to water their horses. Nathan dampened a rag to groom his horse, but the bizarre reception they'd suffered had dulled his mind and he didn't talk to Jeff about what had happened, losing himself in the routine activity.

It was only when they were ready to move out and Nathan checked through his saddle-bags that he discovered he hadn't returned Frank Reed's initialled gun. He turned to Jeff.

'You want to return this?' he asked, his tone sarcastic.

'Sure don't,' Jeff said. 'They weren't grateful enough for us to waste our time.'

'Then what are we doing?' He watched Jeff shrug. 'You fancy finding this Carter Jones in Dodge City and seeing if he has work available?'

Jeff sighed. 'I guess it'd be a start.'

'You don't sound sure.'

'I guess I'm still shocked. They just don't seem to understand Decker's plans.'

'Perhaps they don't, or perhaps they don't burn with the same fire Kenton had.'

'Perhaps.' Jeff turned to Nathan. 'And I guess that, unlike me, you were hoping you could join them and head back to Fort Benton.'

Nathan smiled. 'I'll be honest with you. I was.'

'Why? There really was nothing left for us there. Kenton's dead. We're no longer wanted men. The ten thousand dollars doesn't exist.'

'I know, but it don't stop me thinking about our unfinished business back there. Decker is a rotten piece of work and he insulted us.'

Jeff considered him, smiling. 'Then you're still saying we should go back?'

Nathan lowered his head and kicked at the dirt.

'Not for our benefit, but Frank Reed still reckons this land is worth fighting for.' Nathan turned his steady gaze on Jeff. 'I reckon we should give him a chance to keep it.'

Jeff narrowed his eyes as he looked at Nathan.

'Decker will kill us before we get within a mile of Fort Benton, and even if we do get in there, we got no chance of reaching the tower, and even if we get in the tower, we—'

'I know the odds are against us, but we got to at least try.'

Jeff stared long and hard at Nathan, then looked away, smiling.

'Then it seems we're heading back to Fort Benton.'

CHAPTER 7

'I'll tell you this one last time,' Quincy Lackey said, as he drew his wagon to a halt. 'The moment this all goes wrong, I stop helping you.'

Nathan shuffled his head out from under a pile of saddles on the back of the wagon to see that they were a quarter-mile from Fort Benton. Jeff and he lay beneath a pile of saddles that should keep them hidden from casual gaze and which, if they were lucky, should let them slip into the fort unnoticed.

'You've done more than enough already,' Nathan said, 'by getting us this far.'

'You're right there, but I want us to be clear about this. I'll get you into the fort, but the moment anyone finds you, I'll claim ignorance of you stowing away back there and I will claim the bounty on your heads.' Quincy shook the reins as he trundled the wagon on towards the fort. 'But if I do get the bounty, I'll give you this – I'll throw it away.'

Nathan shuffled down beneath the saddles and lay beside Jeff.

'Obliged for that.'

'And if you do escape with Frank, remember I have plenty of dirty jobs I need doing.'

Jeff leaned closer to Nathan and chuckled with grim humour.

'At least if we get caught,' he said, 'we won't have to do those dirty jobs.'

Nathan responded with a laugh then settled down to await developments. It had taken them a day to reach Hope Creek followed by several hours of persuasion before Quincy agreed to help them. In the end, they had promised him a month of hard work for no pay in return for his help, although they both hoped he'd be too soft-hearted to hold them to that promise.

An hour or two of daylight remained today for them to affect Frank's escape, with tomorrow being the day of the three o'clock deadline. What they would do to meet that deadline if they got away with Frank they didn't know, but they hoped he would have his own ideas about that.

Nathan edged a saddle to the side to let him see the sky and, later, the roofs of the settlement as they passed them by, then the walls of the fort and the tops of the gates.

Once they were inside Quincy headed the wagon across the parade-ground and the gaunt and solid block of the mayor's office swung into view. Quincy stopped the wagon outside the tower.

'Howdy,' he called.

'Ain't expecting no deliveries today,' a voice replied. Nathan presumed it was a guard. 'And I never expected to receive a delivery from you.'

'I've changed my mind.' Quincy sighed. 'A man's got to trade and Decker controls all the trade around here.'

'Then you've seen sense.' Footsteps closed on the wagon. 'But you know Mayor Decker's terms.'

'I do, but if he wants to trade with me, he'll have to consider my terms.' A non-committal grunt sounded, followed by a short silence before Quincy spoke up again. 'Where's he going?'

'To fetch Mayor Decker so you can discuss those terms.'

Under the saddles, Jeff glanced at Nathan and mouthed that even if Quincy had said he wouldn't help them beyond getting them into the fort, he was letting them know one of the guards had left.

'So he's in the saloon?'

Nathan smiled as Quincy relayed the best piece of news so far. If Decker had been in his office, this mission would have been harder to accomplish.

'Yeah, what's that to you?'

'Nothing. I was just trying to gauge how generous he might be feeling.'

The guard laughed. 'I wouldn't hold out no hope.'

'I'm not, but while we're waiting, could I interest you in a new saddle? I got some mighty fine ones.'

Nathan and Jeff took that as their cue for them to try to get into the tower. They slipped to the edge of the wagon furthest away from the tower and out from beneath the pile of saddles.

'Not interested,' the guard said.

The wagon shook and a clump sounded as Quincy jumped to the ground.

'Wouldn't hurt to look before Decker comes back.'

'I guess not,' the guard said after a brief pause. Then

footfalls paced to the wagon.

Nathan and Jeff slipped out of the wagon. They left their guns and the initialled gun behind as they reckoned they'd only succeed with stealth. Crouched behind the wagon, they were in full view of anyone who happened to come out of the stables, but for this risky manoeuvre they had to trust their luck.

'I got one round the back you might like,' Quincy said.

Footsteps headed to the back of the wagon. Keeping themselves crouched and on the opposite side to the guard, Nathan and Jeff paced round to stand by the horse, looking at the door to the tower. It was five paces away, but it might as well be a mile if the guard was looking their way while they crossed over to it.

'Don't like the look of that one.'

'Are you sure? It—' A loud thud sounded and a puff of dust rose above the wagon. 'Damn. Help me get it back on the wagon.'

Jeff and Nathan glanced at each other, their nods confirming that they couldn't be cautious by checking that the guard had bent over to help Quincy pick up the saddle. They headed off, bounding with long stealthy strides to the doorway where they carried on down the tunnel.

If the guard had seen them, he would have demanded that they stop, but they heard nothing, so they hurried on down the tunnel, then side-stepped around the corner to stand in the plaza. They stopped to catch their breaths and calm their thudding hearts.

'Quincy did more than he promised,' Jeff said.

'He sure did,' Nathan said.

Jeff looked up at the tower. 'And now we just have to get Frank out of there.'

'First, we have to get ourselves in there.' Nathan hurried off to the steps to the tower. 'But I'm still hoping we won't have to do that.'

Although Quincy had said he wouldn't help them get Frank out of the tower and he wouldn't wait for them, he had promised them that they could stow Frank away in the back of his wagon. And he had promised to conduct his negotiations with Decker as slowly as possible while not raising suspicion. But as the inevitable conclusion to those negotiations was that they wouldn't find common ground over which they could deal, they didn't have long to effect Frank's escape.

Neither did they have a plan to distract the guards when they left, but they reckoned they'd just have to seize whatever opportunities presented themselves.

They pattered up the steps, coming out on to the space before the mayor's office, and stopped.

'All right,' Jeff said. 'What's your hunch about not going to the tower?'

Nathan looked at the wall leading to the office, imagining the narrow space he'd explored in the tower and the steps leading down then turning away.

'We try along here, or maybe in the mayor's office.' Nathan slapped the wall. 'I reckon there's enough room for someone to move around back there, and that might mean there's a second way in.'

He ran his gaze down the wall, hoping to see a grille that he'd missed earlier and so a second entrance into the prison behind the wall. He couldn't see one, but when he raised his gaze to the ceiling, he saw that there were small holes at regular intervals along the top of the wall. They were large enough to allow in light and to circulate air, but not large enough to climb through. He pointed.

'That proves the space carries on down here,' Jeff said. He looked over his shoulder at the steps then cast a measured glance down the wall. 'But if there's another entrance, it has to be in the mayor's office.'

Nathan nodded and they hurried over to the door. They had made enough noise to alert anyone who happened to be inside, but they still peered round the doorway before entering then stood beside the door.

Aside from the desk and cabinet, the room was devoid of furniture, but Nathan concentrated on the wall. He ran his fingers along it until he reached the cabinet, seeing that it backed into a small recess. He beckoned for Jeff to help him and they each took a side and strained to move it, then peered behind.

But Nathan's hunch was wrong. There was no grille.

They looked at each other and sighed, acknowledging they had no choice but to head up to the tower and get in through the only entrance. So they left the office and hurried over to the steps then to the roof.

Nathan was about to sneak up to the tower and peer in through the door to see if a guard was within, but Jeff rolled his shoulders and took the lead. He kept himself low, silently padding up to the door, then burst in without warning or checking who was inside.

From behind him, Nathan saw him dart his gaze around the room as he charged in. He followed at his heels, hearing a grunt of pain, and came through the door in time to see Jeff slugging the only guard with a powerful uppercut that slammed the man back into the wall.

The man stood splayed against the wall for a moment, then slid down it to sit slumped. Jeff stood over him with a fist raised, waiting to see if he would fight back, but he was already comatose and he slowly tipped over to lie inert on the floor.

'Now,' Jeff said, flexing his fist, 'that's how to act silently.'

'Sure is,' Nathan said with a smile. He hurried over to the grille and wasted no time in trying the lock. The key slipped in, clicked, and easily let him hoist up the grille to look inside.

With the benefit of daylight he could see along what he now viewed as a corridor before it headed down the steps and disappeared around the corner, leading off towards the mayor's office.

He beckoned for Jeff to keep look-out, then slipped through the grille and padded down the steps, trailing a hand along the wall. Even so, he was more confident walking with the aid of the strong light than he'd been the last time he'd ventured behind the wall. And this time he was confident he'd find Frank Reed.

As he paced downwards, a foetid and animal smell assailed him, as of someone trapped in a confined space for two weeks. The smell grew as he reached the bottom step and he wasn't too surprised when he ventured a glance around the corner and saw the dim outline of a man.

He was lying in a recess, this possibly being the only part of the corridor that would give him sufficient room to stretch out his legs while lying sideways. A heap of straw suggested he'd made his bed here and beyond, more steps headed downwards.

'Frank Reed,' Nathan said, 'I've come for you.'

Frank only moved his head as he looked up at him, his eyes small fires in the half-light.

'You again,' he said, his voice sounding more disappointed than relieved. 'I thought you wouldn't give up.'

'We've come for you and we reckon we can get you out of here. We have the best part of a day to get to Providence, but if you prefer we can—'

'Go away,' Frank shouted, his voice echoing in the confined space.

Nathan winced and he heard Jeff hiss on the other side of the grille to get his attention. He murmured a quick comment that he knew they were making too much noise and he'd get Frank to be quiet, then he hunkered down beside him.

'I've met Nancy. She was upset and I'm guessing she and everyone else back at the Bar T has lost heart. But Kenton never did, and from what he said about you, I didn't think Decker would knock the fight out of you.'

Frank sat and cocked his head to one side. 'You speak of Kenton as if he's dead.'

Nathan sighed and lowered his voice. 'I'm sorry to tell you this. He is. But we can still help you.'

Frank closed his eyes, his mouth moving, perhaps in a silent prayer, then opened them.

'And what's this to you?'

'As I said to Kenton several times – nothing other than curiosity, a desire to help, and I guess pride.'

'Then go.'

Nathan stood then placed a hand on Frank's shoulder and squeezed.

'Don't let Decker defeat you. He reckoned he'd broken our spirits, but he's wrong. You got some friends here who want to help. It's got to be worth getting out of here and trying to save your land. What do you say?'

'I told you to leave me alone,' Frank said, speaking slowly with authority. He batted Nathan's hand away then stood and slapped a firm hand against Nathan's chest pushing him back a pace. 'Do it.'

'I can't,' Nathan grunted, his anger rising now that he was again facing the obstinacy he'd encountered at the Bar T. 'We've come a long way and put ourselves through hell to save you.'

'Nobody asked you for your help.'

'They didn't,' Nathan snapped, waving his hands above his head as his heart pounded. 'But now we're here, you're sure as hell going to come with us and try to save your land like Kenton Taylor would have done.'

Frank turned his back on him. 'You don't understand.'

Nathan glared at Frank's back, his heart racing as a blind and irrational desire to hit this man consumed him. Despite the need for quiet, he advanced on Frank, but Frank turned and it was he who threw the first punch.

Nathan darted away from the punch, stumbling back into the wall, but Frank leapt at him and pinned him to the wall then slammed a low blow into his belly. Frank kept him pinned with an arm held across his throat as he glared into his eyes, the combination of Frank's ripe smell and his own constricted windpipe making Nathan splutter for breath.

'Leave me,' Frank grunted, backing up his demand

with another thrust of his arm that momentarily lifted Nathan off the ground.

'You don't understand,' Nathan murmured through gritted teeth, 'we came under the threat of a firing-squad to get you out of here.'

'And I don't want your help.' Frank roared with anger. He grabbed Nathan's shoulder and hurled him towards the corner.

Nathan stumbled several paces before tumbling to his knees. He stared at the floor, hearing the blood pounding in his ears as his anger brimmed over beyond all desire to act rationally. He'd risked his life to free Frank and he'd never expected this response. Fuelled on by his frustration he leapt to his feet, swirled round, and advanced on Frank with his fists raised.

He ducked Frank's first punch, took the second on the chin, still advancing, then slapped both hands together and with a swinging uppercut hammered Frank away.

Frank clattered heavily into the wall but rebounded and walked straight into a low kick that bent him double. With Frank spluttering in pain and temporarily unable to defend himself, Nathan grabbed an arm and swirled round, swinging him into the wall.

Frank hit the wall head first and collapsed.

Nathan stood over him, breathing deeply and demanding that he get up, but Frank didn't move, lying hunched over with his face pressed to the floor. Moment by moment, Nathan's deep breathing calmed him and he slowly became aware of Jeff demanding that he tell him what was happening and to be quiet.

Now feeling ashamed of his actions, he toed Frank's chest, but only succeeding in tipping him over to lie on his back, his blank eyes staring upwards. Then he slipped round the corner and faced Jeff, who was glaring down at him through the grille.

'What in tarnation are you doing?' he demanded.

'I've already done it,' Nathan said with a rueful sigh. 'I've just knocked out the man we've come to rescue.'

Five minutes later, with Jeff holding the comatose Frank's legs and walking backwards and with Nathan holding his shoulders and whispering directions, they manoeuvred him out of the tower and to the steps.

Neither man knew why Frank was so determined to refuse their help, but they reckoned his rough treatment had so disorientated him he no longer knew who his allies were. So they had decided they would still get him out.

At the steps, they debated whether they should try to get out through the main door or head along the wall. They decided that with Frank unconscious they wouldn't be able to get him down from the wall safely, but then Jeff beckoned for Nathan to be quiet.

Nathan listened and heard people coming up the steps, their footfalls stomping closer. He judged they were half-way up the first flight of steps and two men were speaking – Decker and Quincy.

'We don't have to talk up here,' Decker said as he clomped up the steps.

'I thought it best to deal in private,' Quincy said.

As these men were unlikely to go up to the tower, Nathan and Jeff paced down several steps but still kept themselves out of their view on the way to the office.

'All this fort is mine, not just my office.'

Up the steps, Jeff and Nathan looked at each other and smiled. Despite Quincy's statement that he wouldn't help them, he was again risking more than he needed to by getting Decker out of their way. Nathan was just turning his mind to how they would get past their remaining obstacle, the guards, when Quincy spoke again, this time with a raised voice.

'I know, but the sunlight is harsh and you can't pick out all the details. You'll find . . .' A thud sounded. 'You two, be careful with those saddles. They're valuable.'

Grunted complaints sounded, accompanied by a scrape and this time a demand from Decker to be careful.

Jeff and Nathan had to bite their bottom lips to avoid laughing with relief. Quincy had somehow talked the guards into carrying saddles up to the office and was even letting them know what he was doing.

They would have to be quick as the guards wouldn't loiter in the office after carrying up the saddles, but they now had a chance of getting out through the main door and to Quincy's wagon.

Nathan listened to the group clump up the steps, Quincy again finding a subtle reason to mention the guards accompanying them. Then the group headed to the mayor's office.

Nathan reckoned the guards would only be in the office for a matter of seconds so they risked that none of the group would turn round as they walked down the steps. Their surreptitious actions of the last few days had strengthened their resolve, so neither man looked to check whether the group saw them. They reached the floor, then continued down the steps.

Only when they were rounding the steps did Nathan glance over his shoulder. He saw Decker and the group traipse into the office. Then they continued down to the plaza, across to the tunnel, and down it. When they reached the doorway to the parade-ground, they paused. Nathan hadn't heard the guards following yet.

He glanced through the doorway, confirmed nobody was near the tower, then, with Jeff, he hurried around the wagon. They swung Frank's unconscious body back and forth for momentum, then swung him on to the pile of saddles. Then they rolled into the wagon and buried him under several saddles. Just as they were preparing to slip themselves down beside Frank, Jeff flinched.

'What's wrong?' Nathan asked.

Jeff shook his head then ploughed down into the saddles. Nathan followed him. When they reached the bottom of the wagon, he crawled closer.

'I might be seeing things,' Jeff said, then thrust out an arm, pointing, 'but I reckon I saw someone looking at us from the jailhouse.'

'Are you—?'

'Now,' a voice demanded from outside the wagon, 'what's going on here?'

Nathan winced, recognizing Sheriff Buckthorn's voice. With a quick whispered debate, they decided to stay still and hope that at this late hour in the day Buckthorn would be inebriated and so not search with any care.

Footsteps stomped towards the wagon, then stopped on the opposite side to where they were hiding. The saddles shook and a slap suggested Buckthorn had moved one of them.

He grumbled to himself then slapped another saddle aside, this time towards the back of the wagon. Then he carried on walking around the back, all the time pushing saddles aside. Nathan and Jeff pressed themselves flat to the base of the wagon, hoping the saddles above them would keep them hidden.

Buckthorn slapped a saddle above Nathan, driving his face down into the wagon, but he gritted his teeth and welcomed hearing him pace by. Buckthorn patted one more saddle. Then footsteps pattered away.

Nathan couldn't see what he was doing, but heard muttering and imagined that Buckthorn was staring at the wagon as he tried to work out whether his suspicious sighting was real or not.

'Oh,' Buckthorn muttered finally, 'to hell with it!'

A scrape sounded as he turned on his heel then a crunch that Nathan took for him kicking a wheel as he walked past the back of the wagon. Then he headed for the tunnel and the sanctuary of his jailhouse.

But other footsteps were closing from down the tunnel.

'What you doing, Buckthorn?' Decker demanded.

'Just helping out,' Buckthorn said.

'The day you help out is the day I buy you enough whiskey for you to drink yourself to death. Now that's an offer worth considering, ain't it?'

A peal of laughter ripped out, with several people joining in, suggesting the guards had returned with Decker.

'Then maybe,' Buckthorn said with a surprising amount of pride in his voice, 'you'll have to buy me that whiskey today. I've just seen two men carrying another man and that man looked dead to me.'

'Where?' Decker said, his voice now coming from beyond the tunnel and close to the wagon.

'Ain't that sure, but they headed past that wagon. Actually, I thought they might have got on it, but . . . Oh, I don't know.'

Decker snorted a derisory laugh, the sound coming from beside the wagon.

Nathan willed them to finish this discussion and move away, but the saddles around him shifted position and he felt a sharp tap on the ankle. He risked moving his head to see Jeff through the mass of leather, but he mouthed that he hadn't moved. Then he realized what had happened.

Frank was coming awake and stirring.

'You don't know what you see no more,' Decker said.

'Saw Kenton Taylor when he escaped, didn't I?'

'Only after you'd let those idiots free him.'

'Yes!' Buckthorn cried out. 'I knew I recognized them. The men I saw carrying this here other man were the men who broke Kenton out of jail.'

'Where?' Decker roared.

'Can't remember their names. Might have been—'

A slap sounded, followed by scraping footsteps, suggesting Decker had grabbed then shaken Buckthorn.

'I didn't ask *who* they were, I asked where they went. Now quit rambling and tell me what you saw.'

'I told you. I saw . . . Or at least I think I saw . . .'

To Nathan's side, Frank murmured to himself and to quieten him, Nathan slipped a hand through the mess of saddles and placed it over Frank's mouth.

Decker snorted his breath, the sound coming from behind the wagon.

'I'll tell you what,' Decker said, his voice using a soothing but perhaps mocking tone. 'If you can remember where you saw those men, I'll get you as much whiskey as you could ever want.'

Two steady footsteps sounded, then two quicker and heavier ones, giving Nathan the impression Decker and Buckthorn had shuffled round to face each other.

'Can I leave now, because—' Quincy started to ask before Decker cut him off.

'Nobody goes nowhere,' Decker said, 'until my trusty and noble sheriff shows me where he saw those two idiots.'

Long moments passed without anyone speaking, during which time Nathan was sure they must be able to hear his thudding heart. And now Frank was stirring and twitching his arms as he came to. He even wriggled firmly enough to move the saddles.

'I . . .' Buckthorn murmured. 'I . . . I guess they were in the wagon.'

'*In* the wagon?'

Frank sighed and rolled over, his movement rocking several saddles aside.

'There!' Buckthorn shouted. 'Like I said. They're in the wagon.'

Neither Nathan nor Jeff wasted another moment after that revelation. Together they surged upwards, hurling saddles away as they found their feet. Jeff was nearest to the seat and in a lithe movement he leapt onto it, grabbed the reins and shook them, hurtling the wagon off.

Nathan vaulted into the seat to join him as he pulled hard to the side, skidding the wagon round in a short circle to head it back towards the gates. They trundled past the tower doorway with the group outside the door still not having reacted.

Buckthorn was grinning and getting in Decker's way as he crowed at his unexpected success. The guards were looking at Decker as they awaited their orders while Quincy was doing his best to spread confusion by jumping on the spot and gesticulating. As they hurried past, Nathan heard him speak.

'They're stealing my saddles,' he shouted. 'Do something.'

Decker shoved Buckthorn aside, then pointed.

'You heard the man,' he roared.

Nathan glanced back to flash an apologetic smile at Quincy, who returned the smile and a sorry headshake. Then Quincy shouted at the top of his voice.

'Hey, Decker, I claim my two-hundred-dollar bounty.'

Nathan swung round to face the front as Quincy at last did what he'd promised and extricated himself from their actions.

'Fast as possible through the gates, Jeff,' he said.

'That was my plan.' Jeff glanced over his shoulder. 'But we need more speed. Throw those saddles over the back and lose us some weight.'

Nathan moved to head into the back, but when he swung round on the seat he saw that they were probably already too late. To Decker's orders, riders were pouring out of the stables and heading for the gates, aiming to cut them off.

These men issued forth as the guards gathered their horses and joined in the chase. None of them had drawn their guns, but they didn't need to as the riders from the stables surged in to keep them in the fort. The wagon was thirty yards from the gates, but the riders were just a few yards further away.

'Keep a hold of that seat,' Jeff shouted, shaking the

reins with a loud crack. 'This'll be close.'

They speeded, closing on the gates, but the riders drew level then hurtled into the gateway. They dragged their horses to a halt, their steeds rearing, then swung them round to face them. Five horses stood between the wagon and the freedom of the open plains. Jeff set his jaw firm and prepared to force his way through, but then more riders swung into the gateway to join them, filling the space.

Still, Jeff surged on, cutting down the distance and within seconds somebody would have to relent. But then several men drew and levelled guns on them. At the last moment Jeff tore the reins to the side.

He was too late. The horse balked at the impossible demand. Wheels skidded, then left the ground. Then, uttering a dreadful creak and snap, the wagon rolled, hurling Nathan and Jeff through the air.

Nathan hit the ground and rolled, coming to rest beside the wall, then rolled away from the tumbling wagon before it crashed into the wall. The debris missed him but a saddle landed on his legs, so when he gained his feet, his numb legs forced him to hobble.

He saw that Jeff had landed safely but also in the midst of several saddles, from which he was fighting his way out. But Decker's guards had joined the other riders from the stables to form an arc around the gates, cutting them off from leaving the fort.

Nathan and Jeff turned to run back to the tower, aiming to achieve the impossible and use their previous escape route. But to a barked order from Decker, every guard turned a gun on them. One man fired a warning shot over their heads. With no choice left to them, Jeff and Nathan paced to a halt.

They placed their hands on their knees, taking deep breaths. Then, with resigned shrugs they swung round to face a row of drawn guns. Slowly, they thrust their hands high.

Decker paced across the parade-ground with Buckhorn at his side and with Quincy dawdling behind. Decker joined his guards and ordered them to search through the wreckage for Frank.

Within moments two men dragged him out. He was shaken but conscious and uninjured. He flashed a glare of pure contempt at Nathan. And for a reason that he couldn't identify, Nathan reckoned it wasn't because their escape attempt had failed.

He avoided meeting Quincy's eye after wrecking his wagon. Instead, he watched Decker parade around, enjoying his success as he ordered his guards to take them to the tower.

'Wait, Decker!' Buckhorn said.

'Leave this, Buckhorn,' Decker said. 'I'll deal with these prisoners. After all, we don't want them escaping like last time, do we?'

Buckhorn gulped. 'They won't escape this time and you got no right keeping prisoners. They're my responsibility and I'll decide if they've done wrong.'

'Decide what you will, but I promised these men a firing-squad if they returned. I never disappoint.'

'I will deal with them,' Buckhorn grunted.

Over twenty yards of the parade-ground the two men glared at each other and although Nathan would never have wanted to put his fate in Buckhorn's hands, he willed him to win this confrontation.

Decker smiled and looked around his guards, his flared eyes registering only contempt for the lawman and no suggestion that he'd relent.

'I tell you what – do you want me to carry out my promise of giving you as much whiskey as you want, or do you want to look after my prisoners?'

'Both,' Buckthorn said, still with a surprising amount of conviction. 'Like you said, you never disappoint and you promised me whiskey. And I look after prisoners.'

Decker snorted. 'You are not having Nathan and Jeff and you are not having Frank Reed.'

'Don't want *Frank*, but I do want Nathan and Jeff.'

Nathan heard Buckthorn's emphasis on Frank's name and Decker must have heard it too because he stomped across the parade-ground to stand before Buckthorn.

'What you getting at?'

Buckthorn set his hands on his hips, smiling and relishing his moment.

'You may treat me with contempt, but you've forgotten I worked this town long before you came along and drove me to drink.' Buckthorn chuckled. 'Your problem is you don't know the people here like I do.'

Decker narrowed his eyes. 'What you saying?'

Buckthorn licked his lips then paced around Decker to look at the prisoners. He wandered by Nathan and Jeff, looking them up and down. He stopped beside Frank and placed a hand on his shoulder, the action making Frank lower his head.

'I'm saying you've kept this man locked up somewhere and even had me arrest Kenton Taylor for his murder.'

'Frank wasn't my prisoner,' Decker said, sneering. 'He was my guest.'

'At least you accept prisoners are my responsibility,

but that wasn't what I meant.' Buckthorn laughed and raised his hand from Frank's shoulder. 'You see, this man ain't Frank Reed.'

CHAPTER 8

'Hey, Buckthorn,' Quincy shouted through the bars, 'I can see why you're holding those two outlaws, but why me? They tried to steal my wagon.'

Quincy caught Nathan's eye and provided an apologetic shrug.

'I'm holding you,' Buckthorn said, 'because the mayor asked me to.'

'Do you do everything Decker asks?'

'I do when he asks, not orders.' Buckthorn licked his lips. 'And when he's promised me more whiskey than even I can drink.'

Quincy sighed and turned his back on the sheriff.

An hour earlier Decker had taken the prisoner who they'd thought was Frank Reed away to interrogate him. The determined glare the prisoner sported as he led him away suggested he wouldn't explain himself no matter what Decker did to him. As a reward for his information, Decker had let Buckthorn lock Nathan and Jeff in the jailhouse and, as an afterthought, he'd asked him to detain Quincy, too.

Now the three men were locked in separate cells while Buckthorn paraded up and down, grinning and whistling at his sudden, unexpected change in fortunes.

But as if the mention of liquor had reminded Buckthorn of Decker's promise, he quietened and, with his actions becoming more animated, shuffled around, frequently rubbing his unshaven chin with a shaking hand. After wandering for several minutes and then embarking on an unsuccessful search for liquor, he left the jailhouse, grumbling about unfulfilled promises.

Nathan waited until his footsteps receded before he spoke up.

'We're sorry, Quincy,' he said, 'but we won't implicate you.'

'Obliged, but Decker will release me soon.' He sighed. 'Although only after he's made me sign the kind of deal that'll near bankrupt me.'

'Sorry about that, too.'

'You will be,' Quincy said, shaking an admonishing finger at them. 'If you avoid that firing-squad, I'll find unpaid work for you until you've not only paid for that broken wagon, but everything I'll lose.'

Nathan considered Quincy's firm jaw, seeing no hint that he wasn't serious. Then he turned and headed across the cell to sit close to Jeff.

'You reckon Decker will see through his threat to put us up before a firing-squad?' he asked.

Jeff shivered. 'See no reason to think he was lying.'

Nathan gave an unhappy nod. 'And have you had any thoughts as to why that prisoner wasn't Frank Reed?'

'Yeah, and they ain't good. We've ruined everything we've interfered in so far and I reckon we misunderstood Nancy Reed when she showed no interest in Decker's plans. Someone, perhaps a Bar T ranch hand, volunteered to be that prisoner so that Frank could remain free.'

'And so defy Decker and register in his office before three tomorrow?'

'I guess that *was* the plan. Except now we've exposed it and Decker will be waiting for him to show.'

Nathan sighed, lowering his head in acknowledgement of Jeff's version of events.

'And so tomorrow,' he said, 'because of us, Frank Reed will lose the Bar T, after all.'

'Perhaps we won't have to see that happen.' Jeff snorted with grim humour. 'If we're real lucky, Decker will put us up before that firing-squad before then.'

The day of the Bar T ranch auction broke clear and warm, but locked in the jailhouse Nathan and Jeff could only contemplate their failure.

Their remorse was so great that they didn't talk about their predicament throughout the morning. In a curious way, Nathan hoped Jeff had been wrong in his assessment of the situation. Perhaps Frank Reed wouldn't embark on a doomed attempt to reach the mayor's office later that day and so face a man who was already waiting for him, presumably with considerable firepower at his disposal.

But as the day dragged on each event that they became aware of further proved that their interference had removed Frank's only chance to keep the Bar T.

The clock on the wall by the desk was showing ten when Nathan heard Decker deploy his guards outside the door to the tower.

At noon, Decker came down and talked with Buckthorn, even patting him on the back and smiling.

'How long you planning to detain Quincy?' he asked, his tone not condescending as he treated Buckthorn as an equal for the first time that Nathan had seen.

'See no reason to keep him,' Buckthorn said. 'I reckon he was plain unlucky to have those outlaws steal his wagon.'

Decker nodded. 'Provided I don't find a reason to doubt him, I agree with your decision. If you want, you can let him go.'

Buckthorn shuffled from foot to foot. He had been sober and grumbling last night and Nathan didn't expect him to keep quiet about the non-arrival of the promised whiskey. But he flexed his hands and gritted his teeth, perhaps as he fought down the urge to request it, then headed off to release Quincy, while Decker approached Nathan's cell.

'Don't expect the same treatment,' he said, smirking.

'What you going to do with us?' Nathan asked.

Decker glanced over his shoulder in the direction of the plaza.

'It depends how generous I'm feeling this afternoon.'

Without further comment, he wandered past Nathan's cell to stand by Quincy's cell door. When Quincy emerged, he draped a friendly arm around his shoulders and led him to the door. He didn't look at Nathan and Jeff again.

'I reckon before you go, Quincy,' he said when he reached the door, 'you can distract me with talking business.'

Quincy sighed and slipped out from Decker's arm to leave the jailhouse. He glanced at Nathan and provided a resigned shake of the head in acknowledgement of the disastrous business deal Decker was about to extract from him.

'You reckon Decker's comment meant what I reckoned it meant?' Nathan asked Jeff when they'd left.

'Yeah. If Decker secures the land, he'll be in a good enough mood to just run us out of town. If he doesn't . . .' Jeff glanced towards the plaza and frowned.

Nathan set his jaw firmly and refused to let Decker's threat worry him, but with nothing else to occupy his mind, his gaze kept returning to the clock.

The early afternoon passed slowly until, shortly after two, Decker returned to the jailhouse and drew Buckthorn to the barred windows.

'A whole heap of ranch hands have just ridden into the fort,' he said, his voice loud enough to imply that he wanted Nathan and Jeff to hear him. He pointed through the bars. 'Which one is Frank Reed?'

Buckthorn craned his neck. 'Can't see him. I wonder if he's hiding until closer to three.'

'I'll do the wondering here, Buckthorn. You just go out and find him.'

Buckthorn swung round to face Decker, standing tall for once.

'And why should I? It ain't my concern if he wants to come to your office. My duty is to stop trouble happening, and until Frank Reed makes that there trouble, I won't help you.'

Decker glared at Buckthorn, but then gave a sly smile.

'I still haven't given you enough whiskey for you to drink yourself to death with yet, have I?'

Buckthorn licked his lips, grinning despite the insult, but then his shoulders slumped.

'I guess you haven't,' he said, his voice shaking, perhaps with delight although Nathan detected disappointment.

'I'll have a bottle sent down right away. While you're enjoying it, think about who your friends are here.' Decker turned his back on him and headed to the door, but he stopped in front of it. 'Tell me the moment you see Frank Reed.'

Decker left without waiting for a response and shortly afterwards a guard returned with a whiskey bottle. Buckthorn wasted no time in upending it and poured a quarter of its contents into his mouth. Then he sighed with delight and wiped his mouth.

Nathan contemplated him through the bars.

'Hey, Buckthorn,' he said, 'you shouldn't have taken Decker's whiskey.'

Buckthorn paused in the midst of raising the bottle again.

'Why not?'

'Decker's the reason you drink, but you were starting to get yourself some dignity by standing up for yourself. Now, you'll lose it.'

'Be quiet.' Buckthorn took a swig.

'I won't. Fort Benton needs a strong sheriff to stand up to Decker and if you ain't that man, he'll just get more and more powerful until nobody can stop him.'

'I deal with Decker in my own way.' Buckthorn tapped the side of his nose and winked.

'All I saw was you taking his whiskey and following his orders.'

Buckthorn snorted and paced across the jailhouse to stand before the cells. Nathan flashed a glance at Jeff to be on his guard in case he could entice him to come

136

close enough for them to grab him and Jeff shuffled a pace nearer the bars.

'You don't know nothing,' Buckthorn said, hefting the bottle and swirling the contents.

'And you don't know nothing but whiskey. Throw that bottle away and stand up to Decker.'

'Throw it away!' Buckthorn roared. His eyes flared. His face suffused with a deep redness that was beyond the reaction Nathan thought he'd provoke. Then he hurled the bottle at the bars, the glass and whiskey spraying everywhere. Nathan and Jeff ducked away as Buckthorn stared at the pool of spilt liquor on the cell floor, then snuffled and scurried outside.

'You reckon he's gone for more whiskey?' Jeff asked, batting a glass shard from his sleeve.

'Yeah,' Nathan said, glancing at the clock and seeing they now had less than half an hour before the deadline. 'And it'll be harder to get him close to the bars next time.'

'If Frank Reed is preparing to make his move, we got to do something and we got to do it quickly.'

'I know, I know. Now be quiet and let me think.'

Nathan paced back and forth, searching for an idea that would get them out of the cells. Nothing came to him. But as he swirled round on another tour of his cell, his jacket brushed against the bars and a hollow clunk reminded him that he still had the key in his pocket. Buckthorn had confiscated their guns, but his search hadn't been thorough and he'd not noticed the key, useless though it was to them in here.

Nathan removed it then pressed it against the keyhole; the key was still too large for the lock.

'That won't work,' Jeff said. 'Stop hoping for a miracle and work out how we can create one.'

'And I got me an idea. Wait for the opportunity when it comes.'

Nathan continued to tap the key against the lock for the next ten minutes until Buckthorn returned. Then he withdrew his arm and thrust the key behind his back, but not so quickly that Buckthorn wouldn't be able to see it.

Buckthorn had a replacement whiskey bottle and Nathan's sudden movement intrigued him enough to place the bottle on his desk, then head over to the cell.

'What you got there?' he demanded.

'Nothing,' Nathan said, with an obvious movement of his arms to thrust the key under his jacket behind his back.

'You got something.' Buckthorn rubbed his chin while he considered. 'It looked like a key . . .'

He swirled round and looked for the ring of keys that should be over his desk. Nathan had noted earlier that Buckthorn had placed them in his desk and in Buckthorn's agitated state this must have passed from his mind because he swirled round and advanced on the cell door.

'What you doing?' Nathan asked, his shaking tone feigning concern.

'Stand back,' Buckthorn demanded. 'I'm searching you.'

He unlocked and pushed open the cell door, then advanced on Nathan, who stood his ground. But as Buckthorn continued to advance, Nathan whipped out the key and moved to throw it into Jeff's cell. His movement was only a feint, but Buckthorn followed the potential path of the key and lunged, throwing himself into the cell bars.

That was the only chance Jeff required. He had already tiptoed up to the bars. Now he thrust a long arm through the bars and looped it around Buckthorn's neck. A few seconds of pressure from his thick arm made Buckthorn go limp in his grip.

Then, in short order, Nathan had the unconscious Buckthorn locked in the cell while Jeff reclaimed their guns.

'This key,' Nathan said, holding it aloft, 'has got us into plenty of trouble. I guess it was time it got us out of some.'

Jeff nodded as he looked at the comatose Buckthorn.

'And I suppose it was lucky for us he's the kind of a man who ain't got the guts to stand up to Decker. It took no effort to subdue him. He just fell into the bars.'

'He did, didn't he?' Nathan mused. 'And he didn't confiscate our key. Perhaps he ain't as incompetent as he appears to be and perhaps he does stand up to Decker in his own way.'

Jeff narrowed his eyes. 'You saying he deliberately let us subdue him and escape just to annoy Decker?'

'That and something else.' Nathan rolled his shoulders. 'If you're with me, I'd like to back that hunch.'

Jeff snorted. 'Your hunches ain't been that successful recently.'

Nathan sighed. 'Yeah, but look at it this way – one of them has to come off some day soon.'

Jeff provided a sceptical and resigned nod. Then they both looked at the clock. It showed fifteen minutes to the hour. If they were going to help Frank, they'd have to do it now.

They collected their guns, including the initialled

one, then headed to the door leading into the plaza. They slipped out. At the tunnel to the doorway they darted a glance around the corner to see that the guards were all looking at the stables. So they hurried past the tunnel entrance, over to the steps to the tower, then up to the mayor's office. As the door was closed and the area outside was deserted, they headed to a window to survey the activity outside.

Down below, the situation was much as Decker had alluded to earlier.

Seven guards were at the doorway, the only way up to the mayor's office. By the stables around twenty men were eyeing them. Nathan recognized several of them as being ranch hands from the Bar T. Behind them in the stable doorway was Nancy Reed. He couldn't see anyone who appeared to be in charge, and so would therefore be Frank Reed; everyone was acting casually and showing no sign of launching an assault yet.

'So,' Jeff said, 'how will that hunch of yours help Frank Reed?'

Nathan turned and his gaze couldn't help but return to the holes in the top of the wall. The prisoner who, according to Buckthorn, was masquerading as Frank Reed was now a prisoner again behind this wall.

'Because I reckon Buckthorn *has* been standing up to Decker and because Frank Reed is leaving it mighty late to make that move. And most of all because we'd forgotten what we were told when we heard about all of this.'

Jeff considered, then shrugged. 'We were given the initialled gun and a key.'

'We were, and now is the time we use them as they were intended.'

Jeff started to request more details, but with time pressing on them, Nathan silenced him with a raised hand.

Two minutes later he and Jeff were ready to make their entrance into the mayor's office. They had less than ten minutes before the deadline.

Nathan kicked open the doorway then pressed himself flat to the wall in case of gunfire. When none came, he slipped his gun round the door, aiming generally into the room, then side-stepped in.

With Jeff at his shoulder he paced inside.

Decker sat at his desk, four guards stood around the room, and a thin and sweating man with a leather case clutched to his chest sat on the other side of the desk. Nathan took this man to be the lawyer in charge of the proceedings.

'Nathan,' Decker said, 'I should have known you'd interfere. How did you get away from Buckthorn, again?'

Nathan smiled. 'It wasn't difficult.'

Decker acknowledged this fact with a curt nod then removed a watch from his pocket and set it on the desk before him.

'Frank Reed has nine minutes to show and register his title, then the Bar T goes to auction. Are you here for that auction?'

'If there is one, I am, and I might be interested in bidding myself.'

Decker narrowed his eyes in irritation before regaining his composure and smiling.

'And then you'll have to compete with me.' Decker gestured around at his steely-eyed guards. 'For a man who's facing a firing-squad if I'm displeased with the result of that auction, that ain't wise. And either way, you'll face formidable opposition. I've already bid *one* dollar.'

'In that case, I'll bid four—'

Jeff nudged him then leaned forward and whispered that they'd spent some of the money Quincy had given them on food yesterday.

'I'm sorry,' Nathan said, 'my bid will be *two* dollars.'

The lawyer snorted. 'You cannot compete with Mr Decker. He has substantial resources and—'

'Now, now,' Decker said, cutting him off. 'Nathan has made a bid that's far too high for me. If nobody else bids, you'll have bought yourself a ranch – provided you live to claim it.'

'And provided Frank Reed doesn't arrive in the next nine minutes to register his title.'

Decker glanced at his watch. 'He now has seven minutes to make that claim. And you have seven minutes to decide if you want to live.'

Nathan glanced around the room, taking in Decker's guards. None of them had drawn guns, but each man had the casual stance of someone who was used to drawing fast and with deadly precision. He figured the lawyer wouldn't be a problem and Decker wouldn't have let most of his men guard the entrance if he couldn't take care of himself. But that still meant he and Jeff were outnumbered two to one, provided the ranch hands outside kept the guards at the door occupied when they tried to get in.

Yet the gunfire Nathan would have expected if Frank Reed were planning to show still hadn't started.

Nathan couldn't see a clock and he was too far away to discern the time on Decker's watch, but he judged that five minutes had passed when Decker reached out and cupped the watch.

He gestured to a guard who leaned back to peer out of the window, then darted back to confirm that the hands outside weren't acting yet. Decker fingered the papers on his desk, then pushed them towards Nathan.

'Under two minutes left for Frank Reed to sign these, but it doesn't look as if he'll show.'

'Only because your guards are stopping him from getting in.'

Decker shrugged. 'That's not my problem. So it would seem we will have to conduct that auction, after all. Does your bid still stand?'

'Two dollars is what I bid.'

'But are you able to pay up?' Decker said, his tone sneering. 'Mr Timson here needs to be sure you have the funds to match your bid.'

Nathan reached into his pocket and extricated his two dollar bills, then held them high and spread them.

'I believe cash will suffice.'

'I believe it will. Place the money on the table and if Frank Reed doesn't show in . . .' Decker glanced at his watch. '. . . fifty-five seconds, the land will be yours.'

Nathan stepped to the table and slapped the money down.

Decker eyed the bills, smiling, then leaned back in his chair to watch the final seconds tick away. In each corner of the room, Decker's guards straightened, fingers twitched, and hands drifted towards holsters.

'How long?' Nathan couldn't help but ask, as the guard behind him cracked his knuckles.

'Another twenty seconds before you get what's coming to you.'

'Unless Frank Reed shows?'

'Unless that.' Decker glanced at the door. 'But by the lack of shooting outside, that won't happen.'

'Then I'll get the land.'

'You will, except you'll die before you see it.' Decker picked up the papers and held them out. 'Take them to end your life, or withdraw that bid in the next ten seconds.'

Nathan darted his gaze around the room, committing the position of each guard to memory, while Decker held out his other hand. Then Decker counted down the remaining seconds by lowering one finger at a time. Nathan waited until he was lowering the fourth finger before speaking.

'I can't do—'

'Wait!' a voice demanded from the corner, accompanied by a slam of the door.

Decker swirled round to see that the prisoner was now free and had kicked open the door. He stood with the gun that Jeff had slotted in through the hole in the wall outside trained on him.

'And what's it got to do with you?' Decker demanded.

'Everything,' the man said. 'You see, I am Frank Reed and I'm here to register my title.'

CHAPTER 9

Decker snorted as he considered his former prisoner.

'You're not Frank . . .' Decker winced then kneaded his brow. 'But then again, you are Frank Reed, and I should never have trusted the word of my no-good sheriff.'

'You shouldn't,' Frank said, smiling. 'And now my land is still mine.'

'Like I told Nathan, you won't live to see it. Registering was only half the battle. Now you have to get out of my fort.'

Nathan snorted. 'We've done it before.'

Frank headed across the room and patted Nathan's back.

'And you'll do it again.' He hefted his gun. 'It's just a pity you didn't get the gun and key to me straight off like you were supposed to do.'

'It'd have helped if someone had told us what we were supposed to do.'

'We can argue about that later.' Frank roved his gaze around the office. 'Now, we'll just settle for getting out of here.'

With Decker and the guards watching their every

move, Frank signed then took the papers from the desk. Then they backed away to the door.

Jeff slipped out first, followed by Nathan, with Frank leaving last and swinging the door closed. From within Nathan heard Decker grunting orders to his guards but they continued to back away from the door with Jeff covering their rear and the others watching for anyone risking coming out.

They backed almost to the steps without anyone emerging. Then Nathan heard Decker shouting out through the window, ordering his guards to retreat down the tunnel and trap them up here. Within moments, footfalls pattered down the tunnel then across the plaza.

Frank put a bullet in the door to ensure that Decker stayed put a while longer but by then Nathan could heard footsteps pounding up the steps. Then he saw two guards come hurtling around the corner. They hurried back out of sight before they could fire at them.

With Jeff at his side, they fired down the steps, aiming for the wall. Their bullets cannoned back and forth in the confined space, but the shadows on the wall told Nathan the guards had backed away for only a few steps and several other men were hurrying up to join them.

As if the gunfire was the cue for Frank's ranch hands outside to act, gunfire exploded, but whether it would be enough to take out the guards or would just keep them busy, Nathan couldn't tell. Either way, they were trapped, and already the door to the mayor's office was edging open as Decker goaded his guards on to risk confronting them.

'We can't fight our way down there,' Frank said, dart-

146

ing his gaze down the steps.

'We can't,' Jeff said. 'But if we can't go down, we can go up.'

'Agreed,' Frank said. He fired down the steps then at the mayor's office.

Then they turned and ran up the steps to come out on the roof, but the chance of their being able to make their escape as Nathan and Jeff had done last week disappeared the moment they came out.

Further along the roof, looking down into the plaza, was a line of guards. They were keeping Frank's people pinned down in the tunnel, but the moment Nathan emerged, they swung round and fired.

They ducked, aiming to head down the steps, but several guards were already running up to them. With no choice they turned on their heels and ran for the tower, bullets tearing at their heels.

The door was open. Nobody was within, which allowed them to dash inside, slam the door shut, and take up defensive positions.

Jeff stood before the door with his gun thrust through the grille, waiting for anyone who made the mistake of trying to come in. Nathan and Frank took a window apiece, alternating between standing beside them, then nudging to the side to dart a look outside.

At present none of the guards out on the roof had ventured into their line of sight, but Nathan heard them shouting to each other. Presently, he heard Decker's annoyed tones.

Frank looked at Nathan. 'Don't worry. My ranch hands are coming, and Decker will see sense soon enough and accept that he picked the wrong people to intimidate. We just have to hold on until they can force their way up here.'

'Let's hope that's soon.' Nathan shrugged. 'And I guess this is a good time as any to say we're sorry we didn't work out what was happening here sooner.'

Frank flashed a wan smile. 'I'm guessing you came across Jim Harlow.'

Nathan nodded. 'I assume it was him. Decker's guards had got to him first, but before he died, he gave us your gun and the key to your prison. Trouble is, he didn't live long enough to tell us what we had to do with them.'

'Don't tear yourself up about it. You did well.' Frank glanced outside, then darted back. 'As did Jim and Rory.'

'Were they your ranch hands?'

'Yeah. They were with us when Decker came for Kenton and me. They got away, but I knew they wouldn't give up until they'd found a way to get me out.' He looked around, then forced a grim smile. 'I never thought the first thing I'd do when I got out was to hide in here.'

Nathan and Jeff laughed sympathetically but before Nathan could ask for more details, Decker shouted from outside.

'You in there!' he roared. 'Give yourself up.'

'Never,' Frank shouted through the window.

'I ain't going nowhere, Frank, and neither are you. I reckon it's time to come to a deal.'

'I registered my land. There's no way I'll deal with you now. The Bar T is where your empire ends and it always will.'

'Always is a long time when you're trapped in that tower.' Decker edged into view. 'And your people are going no further than the plaza. If you want to live to join them, you'd better do that deal.'

'No deal, Decker, not now, not ever.'

'Then you get to die, just like Kenton did.'

While Frank and Decker continued to trade insults, Nathan looked through each of the windows, confirming that the only ways into the tower would require considerable courage to attempt. Only the front windows could be reached from the roof and the others had long drops down to the parade-ground. Someone could put a ladder against the wall and climb in through a window, but the only realistic way in was through the door.

He conveyed this to Frank, who ducked down and went over to the grille in the wall, confirmed it was locked, then ordered Jeff to listen out for anyone trying to come up that way.

But before any of them could consider relaxing, Nathan darted back from the window as a flaming object hurtled past his head. For a terrible moment he thought Decker had thrown dynamite in through the window, but it was only a lighted brand. It landed in the loose, dry straw on the floor and immediately started to burn.

Frank gathered up the brand and hurled it through a window, but even before it had disappeared from view, a second brand came spinning in through the window, then a third and a fourth.

Nathan shouted at Jeff to stay by the door. Then he and Frank dashed around, gathering up the brands and throwing them through the windows, while kicking up the feet and stomping to put out the flaming straw.

For every brand they threw out, two came in, and

they soon had to give up on removing them. Instead, they kicked the straw into a heap in the corner, ensuring the brands could find nothing to burn. Even so, smoke soon filled the room and it was thicker than Nathan would have expected the brands to deliver. Then he realized why.

Smoke was pluming in through the grilles in the wall. Someone had lit a fire in the corridor behind the wall and the air whipping along the gap was gathering up the smoke and pouring it into the room. Already the top half of the tower was smoky down to the level of the windows.

Although the windows stopped the tower filling with the choking smoke, Jeff was coughing and finding it hard to stand guard before the door and Nathan's eyes were watering and blurring his view of what was happening outside.

'How much longer before your people can fight their way up here?' he shouted to Frank.

'Soon,' Frank said, pausing to cough. 'Soon. We just got to hang on.'

Nathan nodded as yet another brand hurtled through the window. This time it found the fresh pile of straw in the corner which within moments burst into flames, adding stifling heat to the cloying smoke.

'Yeah,' Nathan said, 'but I reckon we'll have choked to death by then.'

Frank provided a troubled nod, as did Jeff.

'You ready to come out now?' Decker shouted from outside.

'Like I said,' Frank shouted, pausing to cough, 'go to hell.'

'It'll be hell in there soon. I got me a hundred more brands to throw in, and they're coming in one minute if you don't come out.'

Nathan looked out the window to see that half-way along the roof, Decker was lining up his men, taking in the available covering blocks. They trained their guns on the tower door, their stances those of a firing-squad who were waiting for their order to fire.

'The moment we come out,' Nathan said, spluttering out his words, 'we'll be shot to pieces.'

'And,' Jeff said, coughing, 'we can't hang on in here any longer.'

The smoke was pluming out through the windows, but not fast enough to avoid it stealing every spare scrap of air, forcing Nathan to agree. He looked at Frank.

'You prepared to do that deal?' he asked.

'Never,' Frank grunted. 'I'd sooner die.'

'And you'll get that wish in about two minutes if we stay in here,' Jeff said, 'and in about five seconds if we go out.'

Nathan looked around, searching for an alternative. And he saw it. He patted Jeff's arm, encouraging him to follow, then hurried to the back of the tower.

'What's your plan?' Frank asked.

'We just got to get on the roof.' Nathan slapped the window-ledge. 'And I always knew Jeff's size would come in useful one day.'

Jeff didn't need to ask what Nathan had in mind. He climbed onto the ledge. He looked out through the window, then reached up. He nudged his head back and gestured for Frank to go first. Without discussion, Frank climbed onto the ledge. Jeff grabbed him around the waist and hoisted him up on his shoulders. Nathan watched Frank wriggle, then lift himself from Jeff's shoulders, his legs disappearing from view.

Nathan wasted no time in following. He quickly let Jeff place him on his shoulders before he reached up and pulled himself on to the flat roof of the tower. Then he and Frank reached down and taking one of Jeff's hands apiece, they dragged him up on to the roof.

They hurried over to the other side of the roof, lay down, then crawled to the edge. Through the plumes of smoke Frank glanced down and confirmed that Decker and his men were lying behind the projections and so were hidden from the tower windows, but from on high he had a reasonable view of them.

'Your ready to shoot 'em up?' he asked.

'Ain't sure I want to fire at other men unless I have to,' Jeff said, Nathan backing up his comment with a grunt.

'Then remember this, Decker had no compunction about shooting you or burning you alive in there.'

Frank stared at them until he received two nods, then he crawled to the edge. They joined him. Through the thick smoke Nathan looked down and sighted the man furthest to the right. Frank counted down from three. Then they started firing.

Their initial burst was deadly, scything through three of Decker's men. With them returning fire at the tower windows and not at the roof, they were able to respond with another destructive round that took out another two men.

They rolled back from the edge to reload and Frank again counted down from three, but when they crawled back to the edge, they faced a different scene. Decker's men had panicked and were hightailing it across the roof towards the steps. Decker was shouting at them to stop retreating and take them on, but the sight of the bodies sprawled over the roof had spooked them and they kept going.

Frank hurried them on their way with a round of gunfire. Then he swung round to aim at Decker, but the last volley of shots had identified where they were hiding and it was Decker who got Frank in his sights first. He fired up at the roof, the lead clipping into the edge of the roof and forcing Frank to duck. On either side of him, Nathan and Jeff also ducked, stayed down a few seconds, then looked up again.

Decker had given up on getting his men to stay on the roof and was running towards the tower door. The moment they looked down at him, he thrust his gun arm up and aimed for the nearest man – Jeff.

From the corner of his eye, Nathan saw blood fly as his friend took the lead high in the chest, the force of the blow rolling him away from the edge of the roof. With the thick smoke curling around him, Nathan couldn't see whether his injury was serious, but a burst of raw anger surged through his veins. Decker was below him and he reacted without thinking. He jumped to his knees then leapt off the roof.

He hurtled down to catch Decker around the shoulders and send him reeling to the roof. The drop pole-axed Decker and winded Nathan, their guns spinning from the hand of both of them. But before Decker could recover, Nathan grabbed his jacket and dragged him to his feet. He stood him straight and felled him with a round-armed blow to the cheek, then dragged him up again and slammed an uppercut to his chin that had him staggering back towards the edge of the roof.

The anger still burned in Nathan's veins as he advanced on the sprawling mayor. He heard gunfire behind him, but guessed it came from Frank as he kept the guards pinned down. He put the danger they represented from his mind as he loomed over the sprawling Decker.

'I have had enough of you and your schemes,' he roared, then grabbed his arm, yanked him to his feet, and kicked him away.

Decker swayed and staggered back a pace, taking him to the edge of the roof. Only its sudden closeness appeared to snap him into realizing the danger he was in. He righted himself, then stomped towards Nathan, aiming a long swinging blow at his head.

Nathan easily ducked under the punch and came up aiming to deliver another uppercut, but Decker had anticipated the move and he kicked out. His boot crunched into Nathan's knee and sent him sprawling towards the edge of the roof.

Nathan had a dizzying moment of looking down into the parade-ground where many of Frank's ranch hands were peering up, having now taken control of the tunnel. Then he lurched forward as Decker kicked him again, aiming to bundle him over the side. Nathan fell on his chest, searching for purchase as his head and shoulders protruded beyond the edge.

Then Decker prised a foot under his chest and kicked upwards, aiming to roll him. Nathan did roll but he lunged, grabbing hold of anything he could reach, and his hand closed on Decker's calf. He came to rest with his body arced backwards and dangling while he sat on the very edge of the roof. Decker loomed over him, swaying and wheeling his arms as he fought to keep his balance.

'Let go of me,' he grunted.

Nathan looked past Decker to the tower. He saw that Frank had forced Decker's men to retreat down the steps. Now he had Decker's back in his sights, but Nathan guessed he hadn't fired because Decker was the only reason Nathan hadn't fallen. He couldn't see Jeff.

A sickness descended on Nathan's guts as the terrible thought hit him that his friend could be dead and that this man had killed him. He swung his gaze round to peer up at Decker.

'I ain't letting go of your leg,' he grunted, then flexed his fingers, gaining a tighter grip. 'In fact, you're going over, even if I have to come with you.'

He yanked Decker's leg with all his strength, tumbling him forward. Decker teetered, but his foot landed on air and he came falling forwards. He grabbed at Nathan as he fell past him, but his clawing grasp closed on air as Nathan kept his momentum going and threw himself to the side.

Still, he followed Decker in falling, but with a trailing hand he grabbed hold of the very edge of the roof and clung on.

As he dangled one-handed he heard Decker's fading screech fall away from him. Then a thud sounded and an accompanying cry of disgust. Nathan continued to dangle until he grabbed hold of the roof with his other hand.

When he was sure he wouldn't fall, he risked looking down to see Decker lying on the ground. He'd fallen head first and the ranch hands around him were looking at his twisted body with distaste.

Nathan tore his gaze away to look up, accepting that he could do nothing but hang on and hope Frank came down from the tower quickly to help him.

A minute passed and then another. He accepted that it'd take Frank some time to get down from the tower roof while he kept Decker's men at bay. But he heard no more gunfire and he expected that once the word of Decker's demise reached the guards, they would surrender.

Even so, he hoped Frank would hurry.

Then footfalls closed. A shadow fell over Nathan's head and he looked up to face his rescuer.

He had to narrow his eyes against the high sun, but there was no mistaking the large form of the man who had come for him – Jeff. He was clutching a bloodied shoulder and he had to gesture at the following man, Frank, to help him, but he was smiling.

CHAPTER 10

With Nathan supporting Jeff by his unwounded shoulder and Frank at his other side, the group walked down the steps from the roof.

They proceeded cautiously, expecting Decker's guards to be lying in wait, but Nathan was right in his assumption that after Decker's demise, his men had lost heart and had melted away into the fort.

So when they reached the parade-ground, Frank immediately disappeared into the relieved arms of his waiting wife while one of his hands who had doctoring experience sat Jeff down and started work on assessing the damage.

Nathan loitered nearby, asking too many questions and generally getting in the carer's way. Before long, he started to feel superfluous, which was an odd but not unwelcome feeling after being at the centre of everything that had happened here over the last week. But before he could relax, Sheriff Buckthorn emerged from the jailhouse, rubbing his head.

Buckthorn instantly picked out Nathan and Jeff, then hitched up his belt and headed towards them, his jaw set with the same level of firmness he'd had when he'd faced up to Decker yesterday.

'You really did assault a lawman this time,' he said, advancing on them, 'and nothing you can say will . . .'

Buckthorn came to a halt. His gaze took in the scene of several of Frank's ranch hands standing around the bent and dead body of Decker. A smile twitched at his lips.

'He's dead,' Nathan reported.

'He sure looks it,' Buckthorn said, a grin emerging before he forced it away with determined shake of the head. 'Now, how did that happen?'

'It's one hell of a tale, but you got to hear my side of it first. We only—'

'I'm sure it is one hell of tale, but from what I can see, Decker clearly headed onto the roof to see who was down in the parade-ground and he slipped and fell.' Buckthorn set his hands on his wide hips. 'Is that what happened?'

'Not exactly,' Nathan said. 'He was—'

'Now,' Buckthorn said, raising his voice, 'it sure would make it easier for *me* if that is what happened.' Buckthorn looked around and received several nods from nearby hands until his gaze returned to Nathan. 'So is that what happened?'

Nathan blew out his cheeks as he also looked around. Jeff was wincing as he had his shoulder prodded but he still gave a nod. So Nathan shrugged.

'I guess when you look at it that way, Decker did slip and fall.'

'Good. Then I don't see no need to concern myself with this. I got a town needing looking after.' Buckthorn swung past Decker's body, pausing to spit on the ground, then headed back to the jailhouse. But on the way he stopped beside Nathan. 'This is your final warning and I won't say it again – if you ain't got a job by sundown, I'll arrest you for vagrancy.'

'Understood,' Nathan said.

Buckthorn glared at Nathan for a moment longer, then headed back into his jailhouse, whistling, leaving Nathan to kneel down beside Jeff. He learnt from his carer that Jeff had been lucky, as the bullet had only torn through skin, but he would need rest for several weeks.

So after Nathan had given Jeff a relieved slap on the back, they just had to face the problem of what they did next. They couldn't stay here now that Sheriff Buckthorn had told them to move on, but they were unsure where they could move on to.

Before Jeff's carer cleaned out the wound, Frank joined them and provided a possible answer to their problem.

'You boys looking for work?' he asked. He considered Jeff's bloodied shoulder. 'Once you've rested up, that is.'

'What kind of work?' Nathan asked.

'It ain't much to offer after all you've done for me, but I always need cattle-punchers at the Bar T.'

Nathan and Jeff couldn't help but look at each other and wince.

'We came to Fort Benton,' Jeff said, 'to get away from that line of work. We're obliged for the offer, but we want to do something else.'

Frank nodded and moved to turn away, but Nathan raised a hand, halting him.

'Don't be so hasty, Jeff,' he mused. 'We did want to do that something else, but every time we tried to find out what that something else was, we got ourselves into a whole heap of trouble. Perhaps it's time we admitted it'd be more sensible if we just stuck to doing what we're best at.'

Jeff looked up at Nathan. His eyes glazed as he pondered before he provided a slow smile and nod.

'All right,' he said, turning to Frank, 'after due consideration with my good friend, we sure would like to take that offer of work.'

Nathan looked down at Jeff, shaking his head.

'We will do that,' he said. 'But you're forgetting we got to do that month of unpaid work for Quincy first.'

Jeff sighed. 'A month of hard work for no pay, then cattle-punching again. The future sure ain't looking good for us, is it?'

Nathan was about to agree, but then saw the twinkle in his friend's eye and knew he was joking.

'Yeah,' he said, rubbing his hands and smiling, 'as you once said to me. Honest work and no worrying about other people's gunfights, and money hidden in forts, and prisoners in cells, and prisoners in towers is just about right for us.'